LIJNKAMP
Literary Agents

§

Brouwersgracht 288
1013 HG Amsterdam
The Netherlands

Agent :

Jane Conway-Gordon
1 Old Compton Street
London WIV 5PH
Tel 071-494 0148
Fax 071- 287 9264

ACT OF DARKNESS

Philip Fletcher, somewhat exhausted and not yet fully recovered from his latest bout of life-threatening misdemeanours, takes a recuperative, undemanding job at the Chichester Festival for the summer season. What could be more pleasant (he reasons) than to idle away a relaxing few months in the countryside at the scene of some of his greatest triumphs? Unfortunately, his peace of mind is seriously imperilled by the discovery that his most hated rival, the unspeakably loathsome and (in Philip's view) utterly untalented Richard Jones, is also appearing at the same time in the Chichester studio theatre. And when it becomes apparent that both of them are eyeing up the same girl, serious ructions are sure to follow.

But there's more at stake than amorous pride. An undercurrent of sinister goings-on disturbs Philip's rural idyll, and when the object of his attentions becomes the quarry of an obsessive stalker, there's once again a premium on his dubious criminal skills. And in the ominous quiet of the Sussex countryside, the hunter soon becomes the hunted . . .

Another wonderfully funny, satirical and blackly comedic novel from the highly acclaimed Simon Shaw, whose Philip Fletcher series is fast becoming addictive.

ACT OF
DARKNESS

Simon Shaw

HarperCollins*Publishers*

Collins Crime
An imprint of HarperCollins*Publishers*
77–85 Fulham Palace Road, London W6 8JB

First published in Great Britain
in 1997 by Collins Crime

1 3 5 7 9 10 8 6 4 2

© Simon Shaw 1997

The Author asserts the moral right to be
identified as the author of this work

A catalogue record for this book is
available from the British Library

ISBN 0 00 232583 7

Set in Meridien and Bodoni

Typeset by Rowland Phototypesetting Ltd
Bury St Edmunds, Suffolk
Printed Great Britain by
Caledonian International Book Manufacturing Ltd, Glasgow

To Carolyn

A serving-man, proud in heart and mind: that
curled my hair, wore gloves in my cap, served the
lust of my mistress's heart, and did the act of
darkness with her . . .

King Lear, III, iv

1

Sally was washing her hair when the phone rang. She stood still for a tense few moments, eyes closed against the stinging shampoo, ears straining above the whoosh of the shower jet, then relaxed again as she heard the tone cut off and the relaxed murmur of Liz's voice. She thrust her head back into the spray, only to jerk it away again almost immediately in response to a sudden tapping on the glass door.

'Don't do that!' she said crossly.

'It's your mother,' answered Liz.

'It would be. Tell her I'll phone back in five minutes.'

'She wants you to be watching the telly in five minutes. Philip Fletcher's doing an interview.'

'Christ! Give me my towel, will you?'

She was still wet as she jumped on to the sofa thirty seconds later. She wore two towels, one loosely covering her body, the other her hair.

'Don't blame me if you catch pneumonia,' said Liz, edging away to the other end of the sofa and lighting a cigarette.

'Don't blame me if you get lung cancer. Is this the right channel?'

'Yes.'

They sat in silence for a minute watching a man in a red pullover talk to a man in a mauve shirt who had written a book on corn circles. Apparently they contained coded warnings from the concerned inhabitants of Venus.

'How much longer does this go on for?' demanded Sally impatiently.

'The whole programme? Till about ten. It was worse a few minutes ago. They had an animal therapist talking about depressed tortoises.'

The red pullover man cut off the corn circler and the camera switched to a carbonated blonde with an uninfectious smile who launched into a quickfire survey of driving conditions in the capital. Apparently there was a traffic jam on the Cromwell Road.

'That's news?' demanded Liz incredulously.

Another frothing blonde appeared in front of a weather map. She told them that it would be raining in London today.

'That's news?' murmured Sally.

'We'll be right back after the break,' said the man in the red pullover as the weathergirl handed over to him, 'when we'll be talking to two of the nation's leading actors, Richard Jones and Philip Fletcher. Don't go away.'

'You didn't tell me Dick Jones was in it,' said Liz as the commercials came on.

'He isn't. He must be in something else.'

'That's a pity. I've always fancied him.'

'Odd taste you've got.'

'Hark at her!'

'If you so much as mention Jason again I'll empty the ashtray over you.'

'Jason who? I'm talking about Philip Fletcher.'

'I do not fancy Philip Fletcher.'

'That's not what you said last year.'

'I never said anything of the sort.'

'Hark at her again! When you were working with him at the Riverside you kept telling me he was extremely attractive. It's nothing to be embarrassed about. Could be just what you need anyway.'

'What could be just what I need?'

'An affair with an older man.'

'Well there's no shortage of them where I'm going. Ssh! I think it's starting again.'

It wasn't, but after exchanging hostile glares they watched the adverts in silence. Shortly the man in red returned.

'Welcome back. Theatre lovers will be in for a treat this season, when Richard Jones and Philip Fletcher will be starring on stage together at Chichester. Welcome, gentle—'

'Actually we won't be starring together,' interjected Philip Fletcher.

He wore a grin like a weathergirl's. Richard Jones shared it. The two of them were sitting side by side on a brightly upholstered sofa. Fletcher wore a plain jacket and tie, Jones an open-necked (or rather open-chested) yellow silk shirt. Despite the depth and plushness of the furniture neither man looked comfortable. Nor, suddenly, did the presenter.

'I'm appearing in the main house,' said Fletcher. 'Dick will be performing in the small studio theatre.'

'No such thing as a small theatre, Philip,' Jones returned smoothly in his powerful Welsh baritone. 'Only small actors.'

'Well you can always wear lifts, dear.'

'Ha ha, Philip.'

'Ha ha, Dick.'

'Ha ha, gentlemen,' joined in the presenter, in the uneasy tone of one excluded from a private joke. 'Well, let's start with you then, Philip.'

'Age before beauty,' remarked Jones.

'Ha ha, Dick.'

'Er, well, Philip,' continued the interviewer hastily. 'You're going to be appearing in *The Country Wife*. It's a new play, I understand, by one of our more promising young playwrights.'

The interviewer was sporting a huge fatuous grin. Neither of his guests reciprocated. Jones wore an air of mildly amused contempt; Fletcher had settled for just contempt.

'*The Country Wife* is a classic Restoration comedy,' he said with some asperity. 'By William Wycherley. It's one of the more earthy comedies of manners, in which –'

'A raunchy romp, eh?' suggested the interviewer, giving the camera a quick twinkle.

'I wouldn't put it in quite those terms myself,' replied Fletcher primly. 'But there was a strong reaction in the theatre and in society as a whole against the age of Cromwell and puritanism. It was a permissive society –'

'Like the sixties, eh?'

'As it happens, yes. The sixteen sixties.'

'It sounds like you were there, Philip.'

'Ha ha, Dick.'

'I'm sure he wasn't!' said the interviewer, who was renowned even amongst daytime television presenters for his literal-mindedness. 'Tell us a little bit about the part you're playing, Philip.'

'I play a character called Horner, who, in order to get his evil way with the ladies, circulates the rumour that as a result of an unfortunate accident he's become a eunuch. The men then think he's perfectly harmless and consider it a great joke to leave him alone with their wives. But the laugh's on them, of course.'

'Of course,' said the interviewer, suppressing a giggle. 'A eunuch!'

He repeated the word like a naughty schoolboy, sharing his smirk with the camera. Dick Jones leant across the sofa to get in on the act.

'There's nothing Philip won't do for his art, you know.'

'Ha ha, Dick.'

10

'Ha ha!' laughed the interviewer, attempting once more to impose his non-existent personality between them. 'You'll be appearing with a full all-star cast, I understand, Philip?'

'Yes, it's a wonderful cast. We've got Roy Power and the lovely Dawn Allen, whom I've known for years, and we're very privileged to have dear Antonia Lynn doing a cameo.'

'And you've got some rising young stars as well, haven't you?'

'Oh yes, we've got young Robert Hammond . . .'

'One for the ladies!' said the presenter with a confidential wink to camera.

Fletcher made no answer. Perhaps he was of the opinion that one for the ladies might be observed rather closer to home. Jones, preening impatiently on the sofa beside him, possibly thought so too. The interviewer glanced surreptitiously at his notes.

'And haven't you also got Sally Blair, the star of *Paramedics*?'

'Oh yes,' replied Fletcher. 'The eponymous country wife herself. I've worked with her before, she's one of our finest young actresses.'

Liz nudged Sally with her foot and, when she was sure she had her attention, pretended to be vomiting into the ashtray.

'One for the gentleman, I think,' contributed Dick Jones smoothly.

Sally made a quick gagging mime of her own. Liz eyed her narrowly.

'Aye, aye. Bet he fancies you.'

'How many older men are you trying to fix me up with?'

'If you get off with Dick Jones while you're down there, promise you'll tell me afterwards.'

'Why on earth should I get off with Dick Jones? And why, if I did, should I tell you about it?'

11

'So I can sell the story to the *News of the World*.'

'Oh, do be quiet, they may be talking about me.'

But they weren't. Instead they were talking about the production in which Dick Jones would be appearing. It was called *Right or Wrong*, and was the new play which the interviewer had confused with *The Country Wife*.

'It's set in Oxford during the thirties,' Jones explained, 'the time of Munich, appeasement in the air. It's a riveting dramatic debate on the themes of tyranny and compromise, complicated in my case by the subtle but unstated implication that my character may be a Soviet agent.'

'So it's like *Brideshead Revisited*, is it?' asked the interviewer.

'I'm sorry?' said Jones, nonplussed.

'Set in Oxford,' returned the interviewer confidently. 'Like *Brideshead*.'

'Well, in the same way that *Rob Roy* is like *Macbeth*.'

'Very witty, Dick. Ha ha.'

'Ha ha, Philip.'

'Er, right,' said the interviewer, like a bantam wrestler butting in on a heavyweight tag contest. 'So you're playing a student, are you, Dick?'

'No. A Fellow of All Souls.'

'Dick's a little too old to be playing a student,' contributed Philip Fletcher.

'And you're a little too old to be playing Horner,' snapped back Jones sharply.

The remark stung. Fletcher looked as if he were trying to reply, but his lips framed only air. Jones ignored him grandly.

'The more time I spend in the theatre the more I find it's the new work that most attracts me. I feel as an actor that I'm probably reaching my prime, and I think I can best exploit that by creating invigorating new roles rather than reinterpreting the old classics.'

'If that's meant –' started Fletcher, but the interviewer cut him off.

'I'm sorry, gentlemen, that's all we've got time for. When are you opening in Chichester?'

'First week in May,' answered Jones.

'I'm sure it'll be a huge success. Best of luck to both of you. We've got to take a short break now, but don't go away because we'll be right back with our top ten tips on things you never knew you could do with a microwave.'

Sally pressed the off button on the remote control. Liz giggled.

'Don't think those two'll be sending each other good luck cards.'

'No,' Sally agreed. 'It'd be less break a leg than break a neck.'

'Your man had the worst of it, I thought.'

'He's not my man, Liz dear, we're just appearing together.'

'I don't think that's the tone of voice you should adopt towards someone who's just called you one of our finest young actresses on live TV.'

'That was just professional courtesy.'

'It's more than he would have said for Dick Jones.'

'By no stretch of the imagination could Dick Jones be described as a fine young actress.'

'Ha ha, Sally.'

'Ha ha, Liz.'

'Stop it! We're sounding like them.'

They burst into laughter. For a moment they didn't hear the telephone.

'I'll get it,' offered Sally, reaching down into the crack between the sofa cushions which had been the handset's last resting place. 'It'll only be Mum.'

She took a deep breath to quell her laughter, then pressed the talk button.

'Hello?'

There was no answer.

'Mum? Is that you?'

Still no answer. She was just thinking that the line must be dead, when she heard breathing. She slammed down the phone violently.

Liz had taken longer to stop laughing. She stopped now.

'It's not the heavy breather again?'

Sally nodded.

'Ring 1471.'

'It won't work.'

'Ring it anyway. Quick!'

Sally dialled 1471, the call-trace number.

'Nothing. He knows that little trick. Or he's in a phone box.'

'You're going to have to call the police.'

'No.'

'It's getting on my nerves too, Sal. You're not the only one who has to live with it.'

'Then you call the police.'

'Are you frightened they'll find out it's Jason?'

'It isn't.'

'Oh yeah?'

'Look, Jason may be a creep, but he wouldn't do something like this. I'm sorry, but I don't trust the police. I know it would get leaked somehow, there'd be stories in the tabloids. We can both live without that sort of publicity.'

'I'm not sure we can both live with this sort of harassment.'

'I'm sorry, Liz.'

'We'd better change the number.'

'Yes. We're both away from next week, we'll hardly be here the whole of the summer. If changing the number doesn't shake him, he'll get bored and give up.'

'You hope.'

'I hope. Now do you want me to –'

The phone rang. They both stared silently at the handset, now lying on the cushion between them.

'Let it ring,' said Sally.

'It might be my agent.'

Liz hesitated for a moment, then snatched up the phone belligerently.

'Hello?' she barked. She listened. Straining a polite smile she passed the handset over to Sally. 'It's your mother.'

Liz left her to it and went to make coffee. There was no milk.

'Just popping out to the shop,' she called over her shoulder from the front door. 'If my agent calls, I'll be back in a minute.'

She was gone for a quarter of an hour, and when she got back she found Sally still on the phone. The conversation showed no signs of abating even by the time Liz had made the coffee.

'I've really got to go now, Mum,' said Sally desperately. 'God! I've just seen the time! I'm late for an appointment, must dash, really dash, speak to you soon, lots of love – yes, yes, I'm afraid I haven't got time – yes, I promise I will, BYE!'

Sally tossed the phone back into its accustomed resting place between the sofa cushions and passed the back of her hand across her forehead in a theatrical gesture of exhaustion.

'I'll get on to the phone people today,' said Liz, handing Sally her coffee. 'Only one little problem, you know.'

'What's that?'

'How on earth do we prevent your mother from getting the new number?'

2

Sally had spent the day before she was due to go down to Chichester shopping, mostly for summer clothes. With her, shopping and indecision had always gone hand in hand, and the business took much longer than she might have hoped, though in truth no longer than experience dictated. It was evening by the time she got home, displaying the logos of Kookaï and Gap prominently to the world, and Liz was back from her temping job. At least, the lights were all on. As she came up the stairs to their first-floor flat Sally was surprised to see her friend crouching outside in the hallway, her back to the wall beside the open door, smoking furiously.

'Why, Liz . . . what's wrong?'

That something was wrong was not to be doubted. The piles of randomly flicked ash and the tight drawn face were mutely eloquent. Liz jumped, like a startled animal.

'Sal . . . it's okay, I've called the police, they said they'd only be a few minutes. I'm surprised they're not here already.'

'The police? What's going on?'

'We've been burgled.'

Sally dropped her shopping in the hallway and ran on into the flat. Liz tried to grab her arm as she passed.

'They said not to touch anything.'

'Sod that! What have they taken?'

She paused, out of breath, just inside the threshold. Her

eyes darted wildly over their living room, over the chairs, the sofa, the TV, the hi-fi . . . It was all there, as far as she could see nothing had been touched. She took a step further into the room. She could see into their kitchen now. It was spotless, untouched. The door to Liz's bedroom was closed. Her own, on the opposite side of the room, was open. She hadn't left it open when she'd gone out.

'Don't go in, please,' Liz was saying to her. 'You mustn't touch. You shouldn't look.'

Look at what? she wondered, half appalled but too inquisitive to hold herself back. She had thrown off Liz's limp restraining arm and was advancing on the door. The scene within opened out like some macabre tableau.

She stood in the doorway, silent and unbreathing, taking in the details of the violation. Every drawer had been opened, the contents strewn jeeringly about the floor. Her clothes and shoes shared the carpet with knick-knacks precious and irrelevant: the brooch that had been her grandmother's; the shells scooped idly from a Cornish beach. Her letters had been thrown about like so much confetti; her books pitched like quoits into the centre of the mess. Her photograph albums were open on the bed.

Not just the albums, but the dozens of folders of loose prints that chronicled her life and career. They lived, in their carefully sorted state, in the old Welsh dresser next door. They had been found, identified, and deliberately brought into this room, to be added to the chaos of her disturbed possessions. And there they had been mutilated.

At first she only sensed the outrage. She could not see what was wrong, only feel that something about the ransacked heaps of photos wasn't right. She walked into the room, sickening still further at the thought that someone, some unlicensed stranger, had pored over private images and stolen such intimate glances at her life. It was quite as if she had been raped.

17

She stopped at the foot of the bed, her feet trammelled in some loose sleeve of clothing, staring down at the pictures on the bedspread.

'Don't look at them!' whispered Liz hoarsely and urgently from somewhere over her shoulder. 'Don't, Sal, come back out here, please . . .'

She stood looking down at the pictures. In some she was on her own, either in costume or as herself; in others she was with friends or fellow actors. In every case her face had been cut crudely out of the photograph, leaving behind a torn, ugly hole. Her workbasket scissors, used to perform the mutilations, were lying on a pillow.

'Leave it,' begged Liz. 'Come back in here.'

'Oh God. I think I'm going to be sick . . .'

She was. She made it to the bathroom in time, and retched violently from an empty stomach into the toilet bowl. By the time her insides were settled the police had arrived.

She sat on the sofa, sipping bitter coffee, talking to a police sergeant. A second policeman was with Liz, making an inventory. They weren't getting very far. It was obvious nothing had been disturbed outside of Sally's room, and as far as she could tell, nothing had been taken.

'Your friend says you've been getting funny phone calls,' said the sergeant.

Sally almost laughed at the phrase. 'Funny' phone calls; about as funny as a terminal disease.

'Do you think it is the same man?' she asked. The sergeant shrugged.

'Couldn't say, miss. Bit of a coincidence though, eh?'

His tone was relaxed, neutral. What did it matter to him, one way or the other? It wasn't his life that had been trashed. He was so casual she wanted to hit him.

The policeman who had been talking to Liz re-entered the room.

'How's it look, Dave?' asked the sergeant.

'Seems like he got in through the window. There.'

He indicated Liz's bedroom behind him with a jerk of the shoulder. Liz had a little balcony, overlooking the patchwork of small walled gardens at the back of the house. It was in touching distance of the top of one of the walls and they had been warned about its accessibility in the past.

'Will you go through your photographs, please,' asked the sergeant. 'Check if any are missing.'

'Don't you want them for fingerprints?'

The two policemen exchanged glances.

'We're a bit stretched at the moment, to be frank, miss.'

'You mean you're not going to look for fingerprints?' demanded Liz incredulously.

'It's not as simple as you might think,' replied the sergeant defensively. 'It's a question of resources.'

'What?'

'And the crime committed. You see, we have a problem here. I'll have to be frank again, miss. All we've got is a breaking and entering and some minor criminal damage to property. It doesn't even look as if you've had anything stolen.'

'Minor damage . . .' repeated Liz, aghast.

'I know, I know,' he said hurriedly. 'I know it doesn't sound too clever from where you're sitting, but the fact is that once we've got this down on paper, in black and white, this isn't something we can do a lot about. It's sick, you see, but it's not serious.'

'What constitutes serious?' Sally asked with a level coolness far removed from her true state of mind. 'If the intruder had stayed behind to rape me?'

'Oh yes,' replied the sergeant evenly, apparently unaware of any intended irony. 'Yes, that would be serious.'

'Alle-fucking-luia,' Liz mumbled furiously, lighting

19

another cigarette. If the policeman heard her, he chose to pretend that he hadn't.

'About those phone calls,' he said, making a show of consulting his notebook. 'It was just heavy breathing, was it?'

'Not even that. He just seemed to be listening, waiting for me to spcak.'

'And this went on for about three months?'

'Well, it started, and then it stopped. I thought it was all over, but then it began again last week. That was when we changed the number.'

'Did you register a complaint with the telephone people?'

'They weren't very helpful. Maybe it's catching.'

'Right. And there's been nothing since? You haven't noticed anyone following you around, anything like that?'

'No.'

'You see, I'm wondering if it was someone who recognized you in the street, followed you home and somehow got hold of your number. You have been on the telly, haven't you?'

'Yes.'

'I saw you. *Paramedics*, wasn't it?'

'I saw you too,' said the other policeman, grinning broadly. 'You going to be in the next series, then?'

'Aren't we wandering from the point?'

'Er, yes,' mumbled the sergeant, blushing slightly as he engaged in further detailed inspection of his notebook. 'When you were on the telly, did you get any cranky letters, anything like that?'

'By the bucketload. Apparently, getting your face on the box is enough to make half the nutters in the world want to confide in you. But they were all passed on to me through my agent. I sent photos and autographs back if requested, but never with my address. I'm sure they were cranks, but they mostly seemed harmless.'

'Mostly?'

'Well . . . there were one or two that were sicker or weirder than the others. Wanting more than my photograph.'

'Like what?'

'Oh God . . . underwear, mostly. People aren't very imaginative, I'm afraid. I didn't answer those, I just chucked them in the bin.'

'Well if you do get any more letters, please keep them. The other possibility is that the caller – the intruder, if it is the same man – is someone you know. Have you been having any troubles of a personal nature recently?'

'How do you mean?'

'A bad split with a boyfriend, something like that?'

Sally was aware of Liz staring at her. She answered reluctantly.

'Well, my last boyfriend and I did split up rather acrimoniously, but he's not the sort who'd do anything like this.'

'He's a bloody nutter, if you ask me,' muttered Liz.

'Nobody did,' said Sally sharply.

'When did you split up?' asked the policeman.

'Three months ago,' Liz answered quickly. 'Just before the calls started.'

'Thanks, dear,' Sally murmured darkly under her breath.

'Can you give me this man's name and address?' asked the policeman. 'We'd better check up on him.'

'Oh God,' said Sally despairingly. 'He'll go spare. I don't even want to think about it.'

'I'll give it to you,' said Liz. 'He's called Jason Barrington. He lives in Clapham. I've got the address in my book.'

'You said he was a nutter, Liz?' chipped in the second policeman.

'The original fruitcake, Dave.'

Although the two of them had only been in the bed-

21

room for a couple of minutes, Sally noted wryly, that had been enough for them to get on easy first-name terms. Reserve and Liz had always gone together like chalk with Roquefort.

'Don't exaggerate,' said Sally sternly. 'He may have been a pit peculiar sometimes, but he wasn't malicious.'

'In what way peculiar?' asked the sergeant.

Sally shot her friend a warning glance.

'He's an actor,' said Liz after a rare moment's pause for reflection. 'All actors are a bit weird. It's part of the deal.'

'Is your boyfriend an actor, Liz?' asked the second policeman casually.

'I'm single at the moment, Dave.'

There may have been no actual movement in her eye-lashes, but there was a definite flutter in her voice. Despite the situation, Sally could not quite rein in a smile.

'You need a decent lock on that back window,' said Dave helpfully. 'Get that sorted and there's no easy way in. You're going away soon, aren't you?'

'Tomorrow. To Chichester. Though maybe I'll be back some weekends. Liz isn't off till next week.'

'To Manchester,' Liz said mechanically, 'the Library.'

'Long way to go for a book,' said the sergeant pleasantly.

'It's a theatre.'

'And will you be back weekends?' asked Dave.

'As much as possible.'

Dave looked pleased.

'I'll keep an eye on the place while you're away,' he said generously. 'Give us a call if there's any more trouble and I'll be right round.'

'Thanks, Dave,' said Liz.

'Thanks, Dave,' said Sally drily.

'It may not be much comfort,' said the sergeant, 'but I don't think you're in any physical danger. The intruder didn't lie in wait for you. Instead he did what he did then snuck off before you got back. I'm no psychologist, but it sounds like he wants to remain anonymous, just frighten you a bit or whatever. You might like to think about installing a panic button, though, just in case.'

It was a cheerful thought with which to leave her. Sally sat on the sofa nursing it while Liz showed the two policemen out. There was a flush of colour in her cheeks when she returned.

'Hunky or what? I like the look of that Dave.'

'It was only a truncheon in his pocket, Liz. Look, what I said about coming back at weekends, it's got me thinking. I don't know that I can face it. And I don't know that I can move back in here after Chichester.'

Liz sat down on the arm of the sofa, looking serious again.

'I was going to call a locksmith now. We'll make that back window properly secure. As Dave said, there's no other easy way in.'

'It's not that. Even if we never get any more trouble, no more phone calls, no more break-ins, I don't think I could feel comfortable here again.'

'But if you leave you're giving in to this bastard.'

'I know. But I can't bear the thought of him knowing where I am, having any sort of hold over me. Running away might not do any good, I know there's always the possibility he could find me again, but at least I'd have a chance of shaking him off. I don't want to find myself lying here alone, at night, wondering if he's out there. If you want to stay on, I understand, but I'd be happy to look for another place to share, if that suits you.'

'Of course it suits me. I'll stick with you, Sal. It's just a pity to leave this place behind. We've had good times here.'

'I know. I never thought I could kill anyone before, but if I ever got my hands on this bastard, I swear I could do it.'

'Me too. We could do it together. The Thelma and

23

Louise of the Chiswick High Road. Shall we try and stay in this area?'

'So you can be near Dave?'

Liz hit her with a cushion. She was trying to be playful, but her heart wasn't in it, and Sally's squeal of laughter had a hollow ring. Nor did they manage a smile between them as they set about the distasteful business of sorting out the mess in Sally's room.

It didn't take as long to clear up as she had feared. Although the room had been systematically rifled nothing had actually been broken so it was just a question of putting everything back in the right place. In this Liz proved more of a hindrance than a help, so Sally got rid of her as soon as politeness allowed. She wanted to be alone anyway. She didn't think she could face sorting through the photographs with her friend present.

Around fifty had been mutilated, fewer than she had thought. She had hundreds more; she tried to imagine why the intruder had chosen the ones he had, but there was no discernible pattern. She thought at first that he'd concentrated on holiday snaps and close-ups, but then she found a clump of despoiled production shots. In several she had been just a face in the background. He'd taken three from *Antony and Cleopatra*, including one where she was barely in view, a smudged Charmian looking on in horror at Antony's death. She had always loved that photograph because of the intensity in the actors' expressions. There was Natasha Fielding, kneeling with her head tipped back in anguish, both hands cradling Philip Fletcher's head. Philip's body was bent like a foetus, the neck twisted at a painful angle as he strove to look up into her face. His eyes burned with pain and love. It was a wonderful memento of a lousy production. Or rather, it had been. She threw the ruined photographs away.

Her white Victorian nightdress was missing. She looked half-heartedly for it through her laundry basket, but she knew perfectly well that it had been under her pillow. She wondered what other mementoes the burglar might have taken; she tried not to think about his motives. She went methodically through her things and found that her little Versace black dress was missing. She knew that it was gone because she'd left it out specially ready to go. Its loss upset her almost as much as the photographs. It was the most expensive item in her wardrobe, and had been given to her after a glossy magazine photo shoot. At least it was something else to tell the police about, though she didn't suppose that it would be enough to make them revise their estimate of the seriousness of the crime.

She didn't sleep that night. She had always been prone to the occasional bout of insomnia, particularly prior to starting a new job or opening a show, but even at its worst she'd always been able to manage a few hours. But now she couldn't sleep at all. She got up repeatedly, made herself hot drinks, read and listened to music, yet each time she thought she had tired herself out and turned off the light again her mind still refused to rest. The night seemed arctic in its length. It was a relief to hear the birdsong, even though she knew it meant no further glimmer of a possibility of sleep. She got up wearily at six o'clock and showered and dressed. Her head ached and her vision was blurred. She wasn't looking forward to the drive down to Chichester.

The call wasn't till eleven o'clock, but she decided that as she was up she might as well set off early. She finished her packing and was ready to leave by seven. She was just looking for a pen with which to write a farewell note when Liz appeared in her bedroom door.

'I'm sorry,' said Sally. 'I didn't mean to wake you.'

'It's all right,' replied Liz, shuffling and yawning her way over to where her cigarettes and lighter sat on the arm of the sofa. 'I wanted to say goodbye anyway.'

They embraced. Sally, who had thus far stoically resisted tears, felt her eyes moisten over.

'Take care,' said Liz hoarsely. 'Give me a call, let me know you got down safely.'

'You sound like my mother.'

They effected tired laughs.

'I'll write to you in Manchester.'

'Would you? I'd like that. I want to know everything.'

'Me too. Especially about Dave.'

'If you're not going to leave this flat of your own accord, Sally Blair, I shall have to kick you out.'

'Then I shall go of my own accord.'

Sally slipped her arms through the straps of her rucksack, slung her bag over her shoulder and picked up her suitcase. Liz opened the front door for her.

'Let me know how you get on with Philip Fletcher.'

Sally narrowed her eyes.

'You trying to wind me up?'

'Moi?' asked Liz innocently.

'Yes. Toi.'

Sally heaved her suitcase over the threshold and took a last look at the flat. She didn't know when she would be back.

'See you in a couple of months,' she murmured vaguely.

'Before then,' answered Liz. 'I'll try and get down to see your show before we open.'

'Oh, right.'

She took a step towards the top of the staircase, then stopped and glanced back over her shoulder.

'Liz.'

'Mm?'

'Bring Dave if you want to.'

She ran down the stairs as quickly as her heavy luggage would permit, the earthy imprecations of her flatmate echoing round the stairwell.

3

'You can just about see the tennis court from here,' said Mrs Armitage, leaning out of the window and indicating the rear of the house. 'You're welcome to use it any time you like. That's if you play tennis, of course.'

Philip Fletcher smiled distractedly. He wasn't really listening to her. He was too busy admiring her legs.

'I play a lot myself,' she said, laughing.

'I can see that,' he murmured, appreciating the smooth, tanned backs of her thighs. She was leaning a long way out of the window and the skirt she was wearing had not been designed with draught exclusion in mind.

'You're welcome to use the garden, of course. And you can walk through the woods. All the land is ours, between here and the road.'

'How splendid,' said Philip, putting down his suitcase at the foot of the king-size double bed.

'It's incredibly comfortable, that bed,' said Mrs Armitage keenly, turning back from the window and closing it. She laughed gaily. 'I could almost throw myself on to it right now!'

Could you indeed? Philip wondered to himself. Although he had only known her for about five minutes he was tempted to suggest she go right ahead.

'You'll sleep like a log,' she said, idly but – to Philip – suggestively stroking the tall lamp by the headboard with her fingertips. 'You can't hear the traffic from here. Not that there is any. You don't have a car?'

'No. Is that a problem?'

'Well, it's a pleasant walk during the day, provided the sun is shining. You'll probably want to take a cab back at night, though, after the show. If you'd like me to do some shopping for you, let me know. I drive over to Sainsbury's a couple of times a week. That's if you're one of those men who can look after himself, Mr Fletcher. Or does your wife usually do all the cooking?'

'I'm not married.'

'Divorced?'

'Just single.'

'You surprise me, Mr Fletcher.'

'I surprise myself. Please call me Philip.'

'I'm Jennifer. I'll show you the rest of the flat.'

She led him down the landing, telling off the doors one by one: a spare bedroom, a small kitchen, a large bathroom, an airy comfortable sitting room. She explained how the boiler worked and apologized in advance for the poor TV reception. He doubted that it would bother him overmuch. He said he wanted only quiet, and space in which to learn and think. He would be opening the play, the first of the season, in a mere four weeks.

'Last time I came down here we rehearsed in London, only turned up here for the last week.'

'When were you last here?'

'Three years ago. I did *Uncle Vanya*.'

'Ah. I would have missed that. I was in Dubai. My husband's in the oil business.'

'And is he still in Dubai?'

'No. He's based here. Though he's away rather a lot. I expect you want to unpack and settle in, Philip. I'll leave you to it. But please, if you want anything – anything at all – don't hesitate to ask. I'm just downstairs.'

He saw her to the door, and watched her descend the

stone exterior staircase. She was about forty, he supposed, blonde, lithe and glowing with fitness, despite the three small children she had mentioned and whom he could hear dimly screaming in the distance. It was the country air, no doubt. There probably wasn't much else to do down here except play tennis; and the obvious. He wondered when her husband was next going away. She glanced back up at him from the foot of the stairs.

'If you fancy a set or two some time, give me a shout.'

'Right. Er, I'm a bit rusty.'

'No matter. Any time. I'm always on for it.'

Philip suspected that already.

She went round the corner and through her own front door, which was actually at the side of the house. The Armitages occupied one wing only of the L-shaped building. The other, which contained the architectural centrepiece, an immense faux-baroque dining hall, was hired out for wedding receptions and business conferences. That still left quite enough room for a family of five, as Jennifer had explained, and then some: Philip's top-floor flat had been sculpted out of yet another swathe of redundant space. The whole ensemble was cinematically impressive. Sweeping up the long drive in his cab on the way from the station, Philip had felt as if he were arriving on the lot of some MGM country-house epic. It would have required only the excited baying of hounds to complete the illusion.

He closed his new front door and returned to the bedroom to unpack. He had one large suitcase, plus a briefcase for additional books and papers. He would be getting back to London from time to time during the season, but an actor, like a tortoise, must learn to carry his home about with him. Over his long years of touring he had perforce learnt the art of minimalism.

He kicked his shoes off and lay back on the bed to gather his thoughts. It was as comfortable as Jennifer had promised. He had about half an hour to kill before the read-through started and he had no intention of getting to the theatre early. He'd always hated first days. They were like the first day at a new school, all skimmed chat and nervous acclimatization. The real work only ever began on the second day.

And he wanted to be working right now. It was a big part for him, and an important time in his career. He needed a stage success; his impact on the profession of late had been carrying his own patented brand of minimalism much too far. His Vanya had been a personal triumph, he hoped and prayed that the return to Chichester would prove talismanic. At least he hoped. Philip and prayer had never been a natural combination.

He lay with his hands clasped behind his head staring up at the pale yellow ceiling. Somewhere stage left a gentle breeze was ruffling the damask curtains, filling the sun-drenched room with the garden scents of spring. However the work turned out, this season would have its compensations. He remembered some of the digs he had endured in his time; slums by any other name: poky malarial rooms with sweating walls and stained beds, pre-industrial sanitary arrangements and post-apocalyptic smells; all the glamour of the world of motley. And then there had been the landladies. A semi-mythical breed even in his youth, a race in hairnets more inclined to regulation than the Gestapo. Though there had always been exceptions. He remembered old actors' tales, buoyed with airy embroidery but rooted in truth, anecdotes flavoured tantalizingly with lubricious relish. In the old days the boarding houses all kept visitors' books, and the strolling players would leave coded messages for the benefit of their confrères. The letters LLO in the margin, meaning 'Landlady Obliges', were guaranteed to awaken the interest of sex-starved itinerant thespians. Even better, and rarer, was the acronym LDO– 'Landlady's Daughter Obliges'. Bliss and very heaven to the heirs of Kemp and Burbage.

Not that his own early experiences had provided much in the way of anecdotal material. His youth had been frequently monastic, his emotional life hermetically sealed. And now that he had reached middle age he found it rather suited him. Better to be naturally guarded, he always said to himself, when he had so much that needed guarding.

Not that he was averse to the prospect of some amorous adventuring – far from it. It was just a question of gauging. Recent experiences had confirmed his natural instinct to avoid involvement. From now on he would keep his affairs simple, uncomplicated and strictly physical. There seemed to be a fair amount of potential raw material to hand. Jennifer had distinct possibilities, and so did the cast of *The Country Wife*, a play with a promising number of female roles. A brief affair with no strings attached for the duration of the season only was just what the doctor ordered; at least Philip's kind of doctor (the kind who probably risked being struck off for sexual malpractice). He wondered who in the company was available. Unfortunately it wasn't the kind of information that came with the cast list. Was Sally Blair currently attached? He let out a long wistful sigh.

Philip did not, as a matter of course, subscribe to general rules in life. He had, after all, effortlessly broken most of the Ten Commandments (including the big one) and so had every reason to doubt the efficacy of similar schemes, but one rule he had tentatively formulated was to avoid much younger women. Thirty was roughly his cut-off point. In his strongly held opinion (and Philip held very few opinions lightly) a fortysomething man with a twenty-something woman on his arm risked ridicule, the one thing someone as self-conscious of his dignity as he was dared not risk. There was the question of hurt, too. He had never fully got over Kate Webster, and she'd left him years ago. Kate had been twenty-six when he met her, which he guessed was about Sally's age now. No way should he get involved.

It wouldn't stop him appreciating her, of course. He'd noticed Sally straight off a year ago on the first day of *Antony and Cleopatra*, with her chestnut curls and soft doe eyes, her peachy skin and sensual lips. As a self-acknowledged intemperate lecher he could hardly have been expected not to notice. But he'd never made a play for her, partly because of his personal rule, but more importantly because he'd become embroiled in a desperate secret affair with Natasha Fielding. Thinking of Natasha cued another wistful sigh. Affairs with thirtysomethings had pitfalls and traps too. Perhaps he should formulate another rule restricting himself to women his own age. But no, that would never do; no connoisseur with developed tastes could be expected to limit himself exclusively to the older vintages. He chuckled to himself at the conceit.

A sudden sharp stab in his side made him check his laughter. Two ribs had been cracked during his last misadventures and healing had proved less rapid than the medical forecast. He'd been lucky, the damage had been remarkably light, but he had decided that he could no longer afford to put himself at physical risk. His buccaneering, freebooting days were over. He was getting too old for the kind of misbehaviour at which he had long excelled.

He saw his face in the dressing-table mirror at the foot of the bed. You could tell the flat was leased to actors; it was filled with mirrors. Sometimes they were discomfiting even to rampant egotists. He saw grey in his thinning temples.

'I know thee not, old man,' he said to his reflection. He frowned and watched his forehead irrupt with lines. That wouldn't do at all; he'd be lucky to pull a pensioner the way he was looking. 'It'll be character parts from now on, love. From nobody to has-been with barely an intervening period of brilliance and achievement.'

'Methinks I do protest too much,' he murmured back. He always spoke back to himself in the mirror. Sometimes it was the only way to get in on a decent conversation. 'Look on the bright side. I'll be able to get sponsorship from Grecian 2000.'

'Why stop there? You could become an icon for the Darby and Joan International. At least you know how to act your age with dignity. Look at Dick Jones.'

'Do I have to?'

He'd been trying not to think about Jones for almost the whole of the last week. Trying in particular not to remember Jones's malevolent taunt during that wretched TV interview. He'd asked for it, of course, walked straight into the trap, and the annoying thing was that he knew Jones was right. He was too old to play Horner, he'd said it himself to his agent as soon as he heard about the offer. John Quennell had told him not to worry. It was just typical Chichester casting, nothing to worry about, everyone was always at least ten years too old for their part, it was a well-established theatrical convention. And anyway, he'd be wearing a wig.

'Look at Jones, I say, for the purposes of argument at least. Look at him with his shirts cut to the navel and his Greek waiter jewellery. Mutton dressed as doner kebab. Thinks he's God's gift. Evidence of a Divine sense of humour, more like . . .'

The situation was aggravating to say the least. The timing of the Chichester offer had seemed so perfect: physically bruised but at the same time getting stale, he had need both of recuperation and occupation. Chichester was the ideal solution: country and sea air; a gentle pace; an easy repertory schedule with plenty of days off . . . it was better than working for a living. Nonetheless, had he known that he'd be sharing the premises with Jones he would have turned the offer down flat.

His feud with Jones went back twenty years. Once they'd been rivals in love, or at least lust, but cause and effect had long since become blurred and the particular seemed trivial in the context of the general. Philip had two principal reasons for loathing Jones. The first was that he was an unspeakably revolting human being, a kind of refuse-eating sub-mollusc yanked incomprehensibly out of his proper place in the evolutionary chain. The second was that he was a crap actor. The former may not have been apparent on casual acquaintance, but the latter ought to have been blindingly clear to a backward two-year-old. It was not, alas, clear to that august body of opinion formers, the critics. With one or two honourable exceptions they insisted on lauding his every theatrical appearance, on heaping honours and awards on to the squat, neanderthal frame of the Celtic retard hailed by one in a rash moment of unquantifiable inanity as the natural successor to Richard Burton and Anthony Hopkins. And if all that wasn't bad enough, Philip had it on excellent authority that he was in line for that most supreme of accolades, a visit to Buck House and a chivalrous tap on the shoulder from HM herself. It had been this very hideous possibility that had spurred Philip on to take the dreadful risks to which he had submitted himself during his latest and most outrageous adventure.

'Well, I may have come pretty near to cooking my own goose, but I sure as hell cooked yours into the bargain, Jones boyo . . .'

He grinned crookedly at himself in the mirror. His own knighthood was as good as in the bag, a fact known only to a few, and certainly not to Jones, whose enjoyment of his own unmerited elevation would be soured irredeemably by Philip's parallel success. The fact that he had had to threaten blackmail and commit murder in order to achieve it should in no way, he reckoned, undermine the merits of his case. His methodology had differed little in effect from standard practice. Anyway, all was fair in love and war – and this was Armageddon.

He edged himself forward to the edge of the bed and examined himself closely in the mirror. He wasn't looking so bad, all told. The grey was containable, nothing that a dab of dye couldn't sort out. His salad days might be over, but he wasn't yet past his sell-by date. He had the fan letters to prove it. There was a whole drawer at home full of passionate declarations from complete strangers. He always answered them, but only with bland pre-printed thank yous and postcard-sized photographs depicting his most neutral smile. Occasionally he had been tempted to make a more personal reply, but he was stayed by tales he had heard of obsessive fans, sad unbalanced souls who feed on celebrity like insatiable piranhas. He had met them at stage doors up and down the country, thrusting auto-graph pads into his face, staring at him as if he were a live exhibit. They were harmless enough, he supposed, but the last thing any of them needed was encouraging. He might be in the public eye (and he wasn't going to pretend that he didn't enjoy it), but he intended to remain private property. The world at large was not yet ready for the real Philip Fletcher.

He did some perfunctory unpacking. He found his play-script and put it in his briefcase, along with pencils and today's newspapers. A crossword was as vital as a script during rehearsals. He kept glancing at his watch. He still had time to kill, but he was getting restless. It was funny how even after all these years the first day made his stomach knot up. He decided to go in. A good brisk walk would do him good. He'd been late arriving at the station and running on the platform had given him a stitch. Regu-lar walking would help get him into shape for the hard work ahead. He needed to rediscover some useful vim and vigour quickly.

He tucked his briefcase under his arm and hurried out of the flat. The courtyard beneath the stone staircase was deserted. He glanced through the downstairs kitchen window and saw Jennifer talking on the phone. They exchanged waves as he set off down a gravel path flanked densely by blooming rhododendrons. At the end he turned right, and set off along a statutory leafy country lane. After a couple of minutes he came to a main road.

It was a main road by appearance only. There was no traffic. He walked for a while in complete silence. He was just coming up to a stone bridge over a little stream, and had just caught his first clear view of Chichester cathedral in the distance, when he heard a car coming up fast behind him. The bridge was narrow and there was no pavement, so he stopped to let the vehicle pass. It was a red, open-topped sports car. He didn't really look at either the driver or his passenger, but they noticed him. The car came to a complete stop.

'Well, well, well!' boomed a fruity, round-vowelled voice. 'Looks like half of Chichester is trying to cadge a lift this bright sunny morn.'

Philip's eyes blurred. For a moment a mist as red as the sports car's paintwork threatened to envelop his vision, but he got a grip, literally – the knuckles clenched over his briefcase were bloodless white.

'Good morning, Dick. Earning a little extra cash with a spot of minicabbing, are we?'

Dick Jones gave one of his tight sneer-like smiles. He casually stretched his left arm across the back of his passenger seat in an infuriating casual proprietorial gesture. His passenger, who to make things worse was a very attractive young brunette, said something which was drowned out by a spot of furious revving.

'Must get on, dear heart,' called out Jones in a testosterone-charged growl. 'Some of us have got work to do!'

'Do you have to go so soon?' asked Philip. 'Aren't you going to introduce me to your charming niece?'

Jones's passenger blushed heavily. A mocking glint flashed in his eye.

'You must be getting senile, Fletcher. Don't tell me you don't recognize your ravishing young co-star?'

Philip blinked. He hadn't really looked closely at the young woman. He did so now. The hair was longer and thicker than he remembered it, but a moment's scrutiny was enough to confirm the embarrassing truth. He hoped that his inward squirming wouldn't show.

'Hello, Sally,' he mumbled.

'Hello, Philip,' answered Sally Blair.

'See you in a minute,' said Philip.

'Yes. In a minute.'

Her words were drowned out in another gratuitous rattle of engine noise. Jones put his foot to the floor and the red car shot away down the road, with Sally Blair's long Pre-Raphaelite hair flying behind.

Philip screwed up his nose at the sharp stink of exhaust fumes and swore to himself. When he was sure the red car was out of sight he gave the stone bridge a pointless kick. As soothing gestures went, it was pretty inadequate.

'How dare he?' Philip demanded aloud. 'The rat! She's my leading lady, not his. How dare he!'

It was insufferable. They hadn't even started rehearsals yet. When and how had Jones moved in on the prettiest actress in town? Hadn't he heard of droit de seigneur? Had he no sense of decorum? No, of course he hadn't, that was a bloody silly question . . . If they were already an item it would make rehearsals intolerable, ruin utterly what he had hoped and expected would prove an idyllic, relaxing sojourn far from the madding crowd. He gave the bridge a second, even more pointless kick. Jones had such an invidious way of getting under his skin. Whatever happened he had to keep his cool; he mustn't let his enemy know that he was getting to him. Somehow he would just have to control himself and swallow his pride. Failing that, he would have to kill Jones.

Once, many years ago, he had thought about it. Now he leant over the parapet of the bridge, stared into the tinkling stream below, and thought about it again. It was one of the principal regrets of his life that he hadn't murdered Jones. Which would be the best method, he wondered. Gun, poison, blunt instrument? He liked playing this game, it was his own personal brand of solitaire Cluedo. Perhaps he could lure him back to the bridge and heave his body into the stream. Yes, death by drowning, that was always a winner, though the water here was much too shallow. It was perhaps incongruous, he reflected, to be mulling over images of violent death in such pleasant surroundings, but he found that they rather soothed him.

Besides, he concluded philosophically as he turned away at last from the bridge and, a little calmer, continued his walk into town, everyone should have a hobby.

4

C/O Stage Door
Chichester Festival Theatre
Oaklands Park
W. Sussex

Dear Liz

I'm sorry not to have written before, but as you can imagine it's all been a bit hectic. I'm sitting in a corner of the rehearsal room (looks like a jumped-up scout hut – bloody freezing today), awaiting my next Act III cue. It's the fourth day and we're plodding through methodically at the rate of an act a day (first day was the usual read-through/ director's peptalk/waste of time). If I don't get on my feet again soon I may solidify. Meantime, writing is good for my circulation.

I can't, though, on the whole, complain. Well, I can, and I'm going to in a minute (let me get warmed up first), but there can't be many pleasanter places to be than here in the spring. All those blooming magnolias and all that luscious green space out of the window (fortunately you can't see the car park from here, just the playing fields on the other side).

We've got our own car park incidentally, a strip of land over by a football pitch where we can park for free. Everything v. well organized here. We spend the coffee breaks throwing a frisbee. We're going to play tennis this evening. My landlady, Penny, is a dream. I'm living in an annexe, part of a converted stable block, but I've got a free run of the five-acre garden and I can use the swimming pool any time I like. Jealous yet? There is a catch, but I'll come to that in a second. Remember those digs we had in Darlington? The ones we moved out of after the business with the rat and the leak? Do you ever get nostalgic? Me neither.

So, what am I complaining about? I'm still warming up, I'll leave that for a minute. I'll tell you about Chichester instead. First the theatre, then the town. Okay, number one, the theatre: you've seen pictures of the auditorium, of course. Bloody great octagonal barn, the old hands moan about it the whole time. Big thrust stage, audience on three sides (1400-seater), drop your voice to anything like a conversational level and you disappear without trace. As they all say, it's a challenge. Over the road from the main house is the studio theatre, the Minerva, which is a little gem – wonderful space. Theatre restaurant downstairs, bar upstairs where you can get a drink after the show. Got my priorities right, as you can see.

Okay, that's the theatre. Now the town. This won't take long. Remember the Noël Coward/New Zealand joke? 'I went there once, but it was closed.' Of all the adjectives I could choose to describe Chich, the following don't spring to mind: vibrant, hip, exciting, invigorating, etc. (consult thesaurus).

Average age of population: ninety-six. I daren't go into a hairdresser while I'm here. Blue rinses are compulsory. I'll describe the nightlife on a separate (blank) sheet of paper. At least the cathedral's very splendid. Incidentally, I didn't know that Philip Larkin's 'Arundel Tomb' is here. I must be either very thick or very literal-minded, but I always assumed it was in Arundel. Just as well Philip told me. Fletcher, that is, not Larkin. Or did you guess that?

I'll come to Philip Fletcher in a moment. I have to tell you about what happened on the first day here. Talk about bizarre . . .

You know the state I was in when I left you. I didn't sleep a wink the night before. The drive down was pretty hellish, I was seeing double or triple most of the way; it's a miracle I got down in one piece. I almost didn't. I'd just arrived at the end of the lane where I'm staying, and I was about to congratulate myself on having made it, when I drove into a ditch. Don't laugh. The ditch was outside the house, it couldn't have been more embarrassing. I think I was looking out for the house name, didn't notice the corner coming up and I was a moment late in slamming on the brakes. It wasn't a deep ditch, not even a wet one, and all I've got to show for it is a tiny dent on the bumper. But I couldn't get the bloody thing out. So when I turned up on Penny's doorstep a minute later to introduce myself, the first thing I had to ask was for the number of a garage so that I could arrange a tow. Still, it could have been worse. I could have driven into her wall. She was very understanding. She even offered to drive me into town for the rehearsal, but that turned out not to be necessary. You see, that annexe I'm staying in has two flats, my modest one-room affair in the loft and, directly beneath, a somewhat grander pad rather out of my price bracket. Dick Jones is staying there.

Anyway, to cut a long story short, Dick was just leaving his flat as Penny was taking me to mine. I must say he's very charming. He came out to give me a hand with my bags, was very sweet about my little mishap and offered me a lift into Chichester. He was starting rehearsals that morning too. So off we went in his snazzy BMW convertible. Nice to turn up in style at the start of a new job, the cool fresh wind in your hair and all that. Unfortunately I became instantly embroiled in a fresh episode of the ongoing never-ending zany wacky ever-so-tedious Dick & Phil Show!

I've no idea why Dick Jones and Philip Fletcher hate each other so much. I've been asking, but no one knows. Apparently it's been going on for so long it's just part of the showbusiness furniture. They're like Bette Davis and Joan Crawford in *Baby Jane*. Except that they're both Bette Davis. Well, we were just coming into Chichester in Dick's car when who should we pass, walking in on the side of the road minding his own business, than said Miss Davis Mark Two. Dick can't resist slowing down, where-upon the two indulge in a quick exchange of mind-less peurile banter. They pay no attention to me, I just sit and squirm, then Philip makes some crass remark about me, and I squirm into overdrive. Philip hasn't recognized me, you see, he just thinks I'm Dick's bit of dumb fluff. I would have been insulted if I hadn't been so embarrassed. Talk about getting off to a great start, and it was downhill all the way after that.

Philip, you see, has been dead cool with me ever since, and it's getting very boring. Even to be seen talking to his arch-rival he clearly sees as some sort of treachery, and he's obviously got it into his suspicious little head that Dick and I are doing much more than talking. So I'm the enemy in the midst. Is it absurd, mad, pathetic or what? But what am I to do? He's perfectly fine when we're rehearsing, he switches straight into character like the old pro he is and gets on with it, but the moment we finish a scene he just blanks me out. The only time he's really spoken to me was when he overheard me talking about the Arundel Tomb, and that was meant as a put-down. You know me, I'm hardly a radical feminist, but I do wonder sometimes what men are for. These two are getting on for fifty, remember, they're not callow adolescents, though you'd never know it from the way they behave. Are there any normal, decent, sane men out there? After my experiences with Jason, I can't help asking.

Oh, Jason . . . I've been trying not to think about him. Do you suppose the police have got to him yet? He'll go ballistic. Thank God I'm out of town, away from it all. I feel safe down here.

I'm sorry, I'm rambling. I think I'd better sign off now, I'm about to be called . . . no, Trevor's just asked them to go from the top of the scene again. Very methodical director, our Trev. Not imaginative, but solid. Safe pair of hands. Very Chichester. Whether the play is VC is another matter. It's bawdy enough on the page, but some of the business that's creeping in is straight Raymond Revue Bar. I know Restoration comedy is all about sex and style, but this one's more sex and sex. There may be casualties amongst the blue rinses on opening night. Does that sound terribly ageist? I must be careful in this company, especially as Antonia Lynn is sitting two chairs away. Not only did I think she was dead, I think my parents thought she was dead in their day. They had one of her old movies on telly the other afternoon. Black and white, of course. It did have sound though – just. She's having a bit of trouble with her lines, but she's the sweetest, most adorable thing. Which is more than can be said for our Sir Jasper, Roy Power. I think somebody warned me about him. Was it you? I was a bit in awe when I first met him (his CV's incredible, he's worked with everyone), but it soon passed. Once he was one of that Angry Young Men crowd in the fifties. Now he's just an Irritable Old Git. Drunk, reactionary, can't keep his paws to himself. He is bloody good, though, it pains me to admit. Master of comic timing. I think the audiences'll love him as much as the rest of us hate him. I think Philip's the only one he gets on with. Typical. Rest of the cast is lovely. Here's the full rundown, as you requested:

Horner	Philip F.
Harcourt	Robert Hammond
Dorilant	Stephen (something, keep forgetting . . .)
Pinchwife	Julian Taylor
Sparkish	Mervyn (whatsisname, you know, from that sitcom, droopy moustache)
Sir Jasper	Roy Yuck-Face
Quack	Another Stephen (keep

	getting him mixed up
	with the other one)
Mrs Marge	Moi
Alithea	Maggie Carter
Lady Fidget	Dawn Allen
Mrs Dainty	Annette Thing (barking)
Mrs Squeamish	Marianne Creamer (Cranmer?)
Old Lady S.	Antonia Lynn
Lucy	Jenny Fleming

Great fun playing opposite Julian Taylor – v. camp
& v. OTT. I was slightly nervous of Dawn Allen,
someone told me she was a frightful bitch, but she's
utterly delightful. Bit old for the part, perhaps, but
she's in good company. Look at Philip Fletcher.
Talking of delightful, I can't remember if you said
whether you knew Robert Hammond. Been with
the RSC a lot, you may have crossed over. Tall, dark
and all the rest of it. Very scrummy. Very athletic
too, he's arranging some cricket match against a
local side in which all the boys are desperate to play
(a certain amount of macho showing off going on,
predictably enough). Lucky Maggie Carter, getting
to do all her scenes with him. Mags sends you her
love, by the way. She wanted to know if you still
had terrible taste in men. I admitted I was in no
position to judge, given my own track record. How
is Dave, by the way?

That's it, I've just been called. I'll write again soon.
Believe me, I've only skimmed the surface of the
gossip here. And there's bound to be another instal-
ment of the Dick & Phil Show to report on. Meantime loads of love.

Sal

5

'Sally.'

Trevor was standing at the edge of the taped-off rehearsal area, looking at her. They all were.

'When you've got a minute, love,' said Julian Taylor jokily, glancing at his watch and affecting a petulant shrug. 'You just can't get the actors these days!'

'I don't think we want to hear about your sex life, Julian,' muttered Roy Power, not glancing up from his crossword.

'Chance'd be a fine thing,' answered Julian sadly.

Sally put down her letter and the magazine on which she'd been resting the paper. She folded it quickly and put it in her bag.

'Doing your shopping list, dear, or just writing to your agent seeing if there's any way out?' asked Julian.

'Just the shopping,' said Sally, coming up and linking her arm through his. 'How could I possibly pass up the chance of appearing on stage with a living legend?'

'I didn't know we'd signed up Lassie,' said Roy Power.

'Ah!' said Julian, patting her hand fondly and ignoring the remark. 'And where would you like us, darling Trev, to vomit on from this time?'

'Where you are'll do nicely,' replied the director good-naturedly.

'Good-o!' said Julian, giving his thigh a pantomime slap. 'Then give us a cue, Robert, and we shall spew forth gaily!'

Robert Hammond gave a polite smile. The absence of wings at Chichester meant that downstage entrances had to be made through the audience via two elegantly christened 'vomatoria'. Julian's glee at the metaphorical implications effortlessly transcended the bounds of good taste. That the joke had long since worn thin on everyone else seemed to have escaped his attention.

Robert looked at Trevor and the director nodded for him to proceed.

'But who comes here, Sparkish?'

A motley crew, reflected Sally to herself as she trailed on in Julian's wake, closely followed by Maggie and Jenny. The two girls were wearing practice skirts, but Sally was just in her jeans, for this was the scene where Margery comes on disguised as a boy. The rehearsal space was crowded and confined, and the eight actors currently squeezed on to it milled around awkwardly with their texts in their hands.

'It's like Piccadilly Circus,' quipped Julian.

'Well, there's an original observation!' said Roy Power tonelessly, filling in another clue on his crossword.

'Bugger off, Roy!' snapped Julian. 'You're not even in this scene.'

'You don't say.' Roy glanced up darkly at their director. 'If anyone could let me know why I'm here I'd be much obliged.'

'Because we all enjoy your company so much,' murmured Robert Hammond, doodling idly on his text with a pencil. Sally caught his eye and they exchanged smiles.

'All right, everyone,' said Trevor serenely. 'Let's get this blocked as quickly as possible, then we can all give poor Roy something to live for. Maggie, Jenny, further upstage please. Julian, don't come so far in. Remember, you don't want anyone to see Sally, certainly not this lot over here. Stephen, Philip, if you could find a moment to break downstage when they come in. General note everyone:

47

keep it moving, remember those sight-lines. From the top, please.'

Trevor worked quickly and efficiently. Nobody stopped to enquire after their character motivation and Trevor wouldn't have dreamt of supplying it. He was a supreme traffic director, adept at blocking, a journeyman versed instinctively in stagecraft and utterly uninterested in the theatre of ideas. He saw his job as providing the skeleton, it was up to the actors to put on the flesh. In short, he was one of a breed so rare and unfashionable that encountering him on the modern English stage was only marginally less surprising than meeting a dinosaur in Oxford Street.

It was a complicated scene, full of comings and goings. Stalls and shopfronts, to be manned by extras, had been designed for the back (and only) wall, and Trevor made extensive use of false doors at either end to cut down on long entrances and exits through the vomatoria. Julian, who relished long entrances and exits, sought to retain his own, but Trevor kept him skilfully in check.

The nub of the scene was that Pinchwife (Julian), in order to protect his wife (Sally) from the lecherous attentions of Horner (Philip), dresses her as a boy. The ruse backfires.

'It is all a bit ambiguous though, isn't it?' suggested Julian. 'You know, a bit Shakespearian. Is Horner a hundred per cent sure that the boy is really a girl when he kisses her?'

Roy Power snorted derisively.

'Just because you're a poof, Julian, don't assume everyone else is.'

Julian passed a hand melodramatically across his brow.

'Egad, protect me! My wit faints!'

'Since when have you been endowed with wit, Julian? Don't make me laugh.'

'You need a sense of humour to be able to laugh, Roy. Do look me up if you ever get one.'

Roy muttered something inaudible but certainly unpleasant, and Julian stuck his tongue out at him. The director smiled and looked vaguely at the ceiling. Everyone else looked hard at their texts.

'I think it's a fair enough point,' said Sally abruptly. 'Roy's just being facetious. Horner says, "Who is that pretty youth?" We all know what these Restoration libertines were like. Rochester would screw anything that moved and check out the gender afterwards.'

'Lucky dip!' said Julian, his eyes rolling like a game-show host's. 'What do you think, Trevor?'

Trevor smiled very broadly, as if to imply that the fatuity of the question demanded special condescension. The whole point about Trevor was that he never had any idea about anything.

'Very interesting,' he said without conviction. 'I think it might be better if Julian were a bit more upstage.'

'What do you think, Philip?' asked Sally.

Philip hesitated. Sally stared hard at him, determinedly keeping eye contact. He nodded thoughtfully.

'I think you're right. It is ambiguous. But I don't think we should make an issue of it. The Chichester audience probably isn't ready for a bisexual sub-text.'

The general laughter helped dissipate the tension.

'You on for a revival of *Staircase* next season?' Julian enquired of Philip.

'Only if they can't get Sylvester Stallone or Arnold Schwarzenegger.'

Trevor and the Deputy Stage Manager conferred together.

'It's five minutes early, but we'll break now,' said the director. 'See you all back after lunch at two and we'll go from here.'

'What!' exclaimed Roy Power crossly, finally putting

down his crossword. 'You mean I've sat here all this time for nothing!'

But no one was paying him any attention. Break times were precious, and there was a universal stampede for the door. Sally found herself escaping into the open air alongside Dawn Allen.

'Green Room?' asked Dawn.

Sally nodded. The two of them crossed the road to the main theatre.

'Well done for standing up to Roy,' said Dawn. 'If more people did he wouldn't get away with it. Let's get there before the rush.'

They went through the foyer, past a star-studded collection of photographs taken from previous shows. There was a wonderful shot of Maggie Smith playing Sally's part in a production from Olivier's time. Another featured Dawn looking stunning as Ellie Dunn in *Heartbreak House*.

'Don't stop,' she said, pulling on Sally's elbow. 'It was taken a hundred years ago.'

'You look exactly the same.'

'Don't!'

But Sally meant it. Dawn had an elfin face, big pretty eyes and a youthful bob in her short fair hair. She was in her mid forties, but could have passed for years younger. Sally looked for the date on the photograph. It was twenty years old. Dawn grimaced.

'I feel like Mrs Pat – I used to be a *tour de force* and now I'm forced to tour. Do you mind if we go by the stage door? I want to see if there are any messages.'

They took the pass-door backstage and went to check the noticeboard. There were no messages for either of them, but there was a small brown parcel for Philip Fletcher. Dawn picked it up.

'I'll take this for him. Come on, or there'll be a queue.'

They hurried along to the Green Room where lunch was being served. They helped themselves from the salad bar and took the table in the corner. It was too cold to sit outside, where there was a small enclosed terrace. All theatres have Green Rooms, where actors and crew can relax and drink tea, but few are as well equipped as Chichester.

'Such a civilized place to work,' observed Dawn, with a sigh that must have been aimed at some of the less civilized venues of her acquaintance. 'You've not been down before?'

'No. Have you been back since *Heartbreak House*?'

'Only once. A few years ago. It was a terrible load of old tosh, I'm not sure if I can even remember the title, but I know I don't want to. It's a pig of an auditorium, by the way, in case you haven't guessed. Philip was here that season, doing his Uncle Vanya. He was really very good. Have you worked with Philip before?'

'Yes. Last year at the Riverside. I was Charmian when he did Antony.'

'Oh of course, opposite Natasha. I'm sorry, I didn't see it.'

'You didn't miss much.'

'So I heard. Sorry, that sounds very rude. I was quite a good friend of Seymour Loseby's, and he said, not to put too fine a point on it, that it stank to high heaven.'

'That about sums it up.'

'Poor Seymour. You weren't at his funeral, were you?'

'No, I . . . I didn't know him well, but I liked him very much.'

'Everyone did. He was a scream. Philip spoke at the service. He was one of the last people to see him alive, you know. Seymour used to say that it was courting death and disaster to be seen with Philip.'

'That's a cheery thought. What did he mean?'

'Only that things always seem to happen when Philip's about. Didn't your director mysteriously disappear during *Antony and Cleopatra*?'

51

'Well, yes. It was very mysterious, he fell off a Channel ferry and drowned. But I don't think that had anything to do with Philip.'

'I suppose not. But a conspiracy theorist would be in seventh heaven contemplating Philip's career. He's a genuine dark horse. Quite fascinating.'

'Have you known him long?'

'Since the dawn of time. He was a year above me at drama school. To tell the truth, I always rather fancied him; I'm afraid I go for the anal-retentive types. But don't ever tell him, for God's sake. His ego's cosmic enough already.'

'You don't say?'

'Is everything all right between you and him?'

'Well . . . no, since you ask.'

'I thought I detected a little *frisson*. You haven't spurned his advances, have you?'

'Er, no.'

'That'll probably come later. He's a terrible flirt is our Philip. I think that's one of the reasons he and Dick Jones can't abide each other. Both notorious ladies' men, both haunted by the fear that the other might be the more successful. And they both struggled for years, there's a lot of professional rivalry, though try getting either of them to admit it. Dick seems to be enjoying the advantage at the moment. His career's on a real high.'

'I'm afraid Dick is the problem with me and Philip.'

'Are you having an affair with Dick Jones? I can't blame you, he's very attractive, but that was quick work.'

'No, no, I'm not. I don't think I'm in the frame of mind to have an affair with anyone right now. I've been having a bit of a rough time with men recently –'

'Join the club, dear.'

'– but unfortunately Philip happened to see me in Dick's car the other day. He's realized we're staying in the same place, so he's put two and two together and made about twenty-seven. It's insane.'

'He's odd, is our Philip. Seems so cool, calm and collected, the original self-control freak, but goes into wild paroxysms of jealousy at the merest mention of poor Dick.'

'I wonder if I should tell Philip that nothing's going on.'

'Oh, I wouldn't do that, he'll probably think you're signalling your availability. A more subtle approach is required. I'll have a discreet word in his ear at an opportune moment, if you like.'

'Dawn, that's terribly sweet of you.'

'Not at all, dear. Now don't look round, but he's just this second come in through the door. We'll have to gossip about something else. Who do you fancy in the cast?'

'Er, I don't know.'

'Of course, you're off men, aren't you? That Robert boy's a bit pretty. Mm, if I were ten years younger . . .'

'Aren't you a respectable married woman?'

'No, just a married woman. Philip's looking this way. I'm afraid I'm going to have to ask him over. Oh God, it looks like bloody Roy is tailing him. Oh hell . . . Philip, darling, how lovely. Will you join us? I've got something for you.'

'Lucky Philip!' leered Roy Power, coming up at his shoulder with an enormous tray of food. 'Budge up, then.'

Reluctantly Sally and Dawn moved their chairs apart, allowing Roy to sit between them. Philip took the fourth chair, next to Sally and the window.

'For you,' said Dawn, pushing over the small brown parcel. 'It was at the stage door.'

'Thanks.'

Philip glanced briefly at the parcel before depositing it on the floor by his chair. There was no room for it on the table, which was piled high with plates and cups. Most of them belonged to Roy Power, who was shovelling food and drink into his thin wiry frame as fast as he could.

53

Dawn attempted to lift the conversation over the sounds of chomping and slurping.

'Have you been on stage yet, Philip? I was warning Sally what a pig it is.'

'Yes, I've had a little wander. And it is.'

'Diction!' snarled Roy Power through a mouthful of pie and pickle. 'Clear articulation. All you need.'

'Mm, talking of pigs,' Dawn murmured to Sally.

'Don't bloody teach it in drama schools,' Roy continued forcefully, warming to a pet subject. 'All bloody muttering, method rubbish, TV acting. Improvisation, that's all they teach nowadays.'

'We hardly did any improvisation at all,' protested Sally.

'Trendy teaching, that's what's wrong,' continued Roy, simply ignoring her. 'What's wrong with the country, if you ask me –'

'Did we?' interjected Dawn, fruitlessly – she may as well have lain down in front of a steamroller.

'No respect for tradition. No knowledge about anything. Tell me, have you heard of Edith Evans?'

Sally failed to realize for a moment that the question was addressed to her.

'Have you heard of Peggy Ashcroft?' Roy persisted.

'Well, yes,' answered Sally reluctantly.

'I've just finished working with a girl just out of drama school who hadn't heard of either of them, yet she claims to want to be an actress. They've all got bloody mobile phones.'

Dawn and Sally exchanged blank looks. Roy paused only for long enough to cram in another forkful of food.

'Did you see them at the end of rehearsal? Robert. Stephen, Maggie. All getting on their mobiles. What's is all bloody for?'

'I'm sorry, Roy,' said Dawn sweetly. 'You've lost me here.'

'Gimmicks. That's what it is. What's wrong with the

phone at the stage door? – that's what I'd like to know.'

'I'm afraid I can't answer that question,' said Dawn, looking at her watch. 'I've got some shopping to do.'

'Can't blame them, I suppose,' grumbled Roy, shoving aside his plate and taking a mighty bite out of an apple tart. 'Bloody trendy education system. All products of Mixed Ability Teaching, I expect. Imagine if we had that in the theatre. Mixed Ability Acting!'

'Oh but we have,' said Philip Fletcher, also looking at his watch. 'It's called the Royal Shakespeare Company. I think I'm going to check out if that stage-door phone is working.'

Roy's eyes focused sharply on Philip's plate, on which sat half a cheese sandwich.

'Aren't you going to eat that?'

Philip shook his head. Roy snatched up the plate and put it on his own tray.

'Where does it all go?' Dawn wondered aloud, looking down at her plate. 'I've got half a tomato, if you'd like that.'

'Hate tomatoes,' said Roy indignantly.

'Yes, they are a bit trendy, aren't they?' said Dawn, rising and shouldering her bag. Sally got up with her.

'Mind if I come with you into town?'

'Of course not.'

Philip was also getting to his feet. Roy looked up at each of them in turn.

'Something I said?'

It was a question none of them quite dared answer.

'I'll take those,' said Sally, reaching over for Dawn's empty plate and glass and putting them on to her tray.

'Please allow me,' said Dick Jones, appearing out of nowhere at Sally's shoulder and taking the tray before she could say anything. 'Do you have to be going? I can't tempt you to stay for a coffee?'

Sally blushed. Dick put on his most charming smile.

'Dawn, you're looking lovely as ever. I've just been drooling over your portrait as Ellie Dunn. Of course, I've always adored Shaw –'

'Bernard or Sandie, Dick?'

'Ha ha, Philip. What a delight to see you here.'

There was little delight evident in Philip's expression.

'Be gentle with him, my dear,' said Dick to Sally. 'He's not as young as he was. Don't know about *The Country Wife*, eh, Philip? Next year it'll be The Rake's Grandfather.'

'Ha ha, Dick.'

'Ha ha, Philip.'

'We'd best be off,' said Dawn hurriedly. 'I'm taking Sally shopping.'

'I'm off too,' said Philip.

'That upsets me less,' said Dick airily, carrying Sally's tray over to the counter. 'Nothing personal, you understand.'

Philip did not return his outsized grin. He headed for the door, followed by the two women.

'See you back at rehearsals,' he said.

'And I'll see you tonight then, Sally,' called Dick casually. 'Back at the ranch.'

Philip said nothing, but the others heard him bristle. Dick sat down in his place.

'You don't mind if I join you, Roy? I'm glad to see they're not starving you. Oh, Philip!'

Philip was already halfway through the door. He turned back with the greatest reluctance.

'This yours, old friend?'

Dick was holding up the small brown parcel. Philip walked over briskly to retrieve it.

'Anything interesting?' asked Dick, giving the parcel a shake. Philip snatched it from him.

'None of your business – old friend.'

He tucked the parcel under his arm and exited con brio.

Dawn and Sally were ahead of him, making towards the stage door. He had been intending to phone his agent, but it could wait. He turned right instead, and walked out through the foyer.

He kept on walking when he got outside. He had been breathing contaminated air, he needed to clear his lungs. He strode rapidly over Oaklands Park, crossed the length of two rugby pitches and came to a stop by a wooden bench. The wind was sharp and there was no one about. He pulled up his lapels, thrust his hands into his pockets and sat down. He paused to gather breath, then swore creatively at length.

'This is intolerable,' he muttered angrily to himself when he had at length exhausted his reserve of expletives. 'The mere presence of Jones is making me ill. I'm an artist, it's a question of temperament; my whole creative being has been thrown out of kilter. There should be some sort of apartheid system, to keep him and his lot away from me and mine. Especially Sally Blair. It wouldn't be so bad if she wasn't so damned attractive. What do women see in you, Jones, you odious apology for an underfunded laboratory experiment? The last time I saw anything with as much excess body hair it was wearing a lead and a collar. It must be like going to bed with a Yeti. How could she! If she must consort with someone twice her age, what's wrong with me?'

He got up and paced about on the grass in front of the bench. Losing out to Dick Jones might mark a new low point in his life, but it was hardly the first iceberg he'd ever struck on the sea of love. He winced, though whether at a particular recollection or at the metaphor not even he could be sure. He felt a terrible surge of self-pity coming on. His love life had been a total mess, always. Women came and went like buses, took him for a couple of sops and then it was 'Press Button Once' and off they went.

None hung around, no one could put up with him for long. He told himself that was how he liked it, he liked his freedom, he was one of nature's ruminants, but he was so adept at all kinds of deception, including the auto variety, how could he be sure? A line from Webster came into his head: *we are instruments, not agents* . . . Natasha Fielding was a case in point. He thought he had been the one calling the shots, but he had been her instrument all along. She'd got herself pregnant by him then disappeared to Canada. He hadn't heard from her for ages. He supposed he must be a father by now, a disquieting thought for a man with such profoundly negative paternal feelings. That helped him pretend that he didn't mind, but he did. Dammit he did! Natasha had hurt him, like Kate, like Hannah, like Natasha again the first time he'd met her twenty years ago, when he'd been utterly humiliated, like . . . like the rest.

'Get a bloody grip!' he admonished himself, kicking a loose sod on to the nearest playing pitch. 'For God's sake act your age, and act professionally. You've a play to do, a difficult part to perform. Forget Sally Blair. The world is full of pretty girls. It's just the fact that she's having an affair with Jones that's getting to you. You wouldn't be bothered otherwise, remember the rule . . . God, has she no taste? No, damn, let it go. If she wants to throw away her life, that's her business. Pay no attention, it doesn't concern you. I feel sorry for the poor girl. Forget it. Forget Jones. He's just a pimple on the theatrical fundament, not worth thinking about. Let them get on with it, it doesn't concern you and it doesn't bother you, right? Be completely cool. Give him no reason at all to gloat. You're not even remotely interested in Sally, you couldn't care less. Has she any reason to think otherwise? No, I don't think there's been anything in my behaviour to make her think I'm in any way out of sorts. Well let's keep it that way.

Good, I'm glad that's clear. It's time I was getting back to rehearsal.'

He was about to set off when he noticed the small brown parcel. He'd left it on the bench. It hadn't been stamped, instead a bold black felt-tip scrawl across the top proclaimed that it had been delivered 'By Hand'. He didn't recognize the writing and there was no sender's name on the back. He tore open the heavily Sellotaped ends and unfolded the brown paper. Within he discovered a scented letter on a single sheet of paper, and a pair of ladies' red silk knickers.

He held up the knickers and inspected them with some bemusement. They were far from skimpy; indeed, he was not surprised to see that the label said 'Extra Large'. It also proclaimed the name of a well-known chain of sex shops. On closer inspection he noticed that the knickers were crotchless. He opened the letter.

Heron Farm
Goodwood
West Sussex

Dear darling Philip

What a heartless naughty boy you are! Fancy being down in Chichester the best part of a week without getting in touch. Not even any flowers? How could you! So, I'm just sending you a little something to remember me by, and to get you warmed up! I wore these for you last time, remember? I'm sure you do, you were so passionate, so mad, bad and dangerous to know! How we made love all night, I'll never forget – all those naughty things you said to me, you naughty, saucy man! I know you have other women, but I don't worry about them. I know that I am your one true love, I know that you will always come back to me. Come back soon, my door is always open for you.

Your ever-faithful darling,

Olive

Philip read the letter through again, examined the knickers, reread the letter, re-examined the knickers, then re-reread the letter. He was none the wiser.

'Olive?'

He didn't recall the name from his collected fan mail. He gave the knicker elastic a bemused pull. Extra Large seemed a bit of an understatement. The sight of Olive, whoever she was, in this particular pair of crotchless briefs was not one he would have forgotten in a hurry.

'Oh well,' he murmured to himself. 'The price of fame, I guess.'

He chuckled to himself as he folded the knickers and put them away in his pocket. They would make an excellent addition to his collection. He ought to get them framed, maybe make a donation to the Theatre Museum in Covent Garden. He just hoped that he wouldn't bump into their owner.

He returned to the rehearsal room in a surprisingly upbeat mood.

6

The track that led down to the cottage was no more than a sequence of potholes, coarsely rutted. The first and only time he'd tried to drive it he'd dented his new exhaust. Thereafter he'd just left his van outside the farmhouse, avoiding the slippery morass left by generations of tractors. Olive had told him that he could do that.

As he was edging the van up on to the grass bank by the gate he noticed Olive through her kitchen window, waving to draw his attention. By the time he had parked the van and locked it she had appeared at her front door. She called to him over the wall.

'Come and have some tea,' she said eagerly. 'Or something stronger, if you'd rather.'

'Tea would be nice,' he said, though he didn't mean it. He unlocked his van again and put his shopping, which was in a white plastic carrier bag, back on the driver's seat. He didn't want to talk to Olive, but he felt he had to make the effort. This was only his second day there, after all. He opened the gate and went into the farmyard.

He followed her through the dark, stone-floored hallway and into the scarcely less gloomy kitchen. She lifted an old black kettle off the Aga.

'Just boiled,' she said, heaping tea into the pot. 'Hope you like it strong.'

He found somewhere to sit that wasn't covered with newspapers. Cat hairs were everywhere. One whole corner was filled with dog and cat bowls. The room stank of old meat.

'Here's sugar and milk,' said Olive, carrying over a tray containing the pot and some unmatched crockery. 'We'll let it brew for a minute.'

She pulled out a chair opposite his, startling a sleeping white cat which awoke bristling and swept crossly out of the room. She leant across the table towards him, her eyes bright and eager. She was trembling. He could see how the flesh strained at her collar, at her sleeves, how the fat body stretched the fabric of her dress. Looking at her made him feel ill, so he looked instead out of the window. She disgusted him.

'Well?' she demanded. 'Did you deliver it okay?'

'Like you said, Olive. I left it at the stage door.'

She let out a sigh, leant her elbows on the table and cupped her face in her hands, the flesh spilling through her fingers. She half-closed her eyes and smiled dreamily.

'He'll have got it by now then. He'll be round later, I expect. I hope you won't think me rude if I ask you to leave when he comes.'

'No. I've got to go out anyway.'

'Have your tea first, though. I'm sure there'll be time. He'll only just have finished rehearsals. He likes to unwind a bit first, before coming round. It's very hard being an actor, you know. He needs time to stop pretending that he's someone else, to remember to be himself again. Sometimes he forgets to do that, you know. He gets so involved in what he's doing, his concentration is so incredible, he forgets who people are, even me sometimes. I know it seems ridiculous, but he does, he just looks straight through me, as if he doesn't know me. It's hard to believe, but it's true. Do you take sugar?'

He nodded, took the bowl from her and scooped two heaped teaspoons into his mug. He sneezed.

'Want a tissue?' she asked. He shook his head. She

62

poured the tea. 'I hope that's not too strong for you. You can have more milk if you like.'

'That's fine. As it comes.'

'You don't mind, eh? As long as it's warm and wet!'

He smiled back emptily. It's all right, he told himself, gripping the blue china mug tight, imagining the fingers round the handle were round her throat – it's all right, just play along, just grin and bear it.

'When did you say your girlfriend was coming down?'

'She's not my girlfriend, she's my fiancée.'

'Ah!' said Olive, simpering and beaming. 'Isn't that nice! When's the happy day?'

'We . . . we don't know, we haven't decided.'

He shifted in his seat. He was feeling uncomfortable. He scooped a few more sugar grains into his mug and stirred the spoon around purposefully. He kept his eyes down. He wouldn't look at her.

'That is nice,' she was saying. 'Will it be church, or don't you know? I know it's none of my business, but I do think church is best. It's proper, somehow, you know what I mean? What's she called?'

He stirred the spoon quickly. He was aware of her leaning towards him, probing him with her stupid chat, wanting to drag things out.

'What's her name?'

He picked up his mug in both hands, held it to his face. His mouth hidden from her, he moved his lips in silent curses.

'What did you say her name was?'

Shut up, said his silent lips, *shut up, you fat bitch*.

'Can you keep a secret?' he said. He looked into her big, dull, stupid eyes and feigned intimacy.

'A secret?' she repeated.

'Yes. We're eloping, that's what it's about, you see. Her people don't want it. She's told them she won't see me again, but she's going to, of course, as soon as she can get away. But I shouldn't tell anyone, you see, not even her. It's secret.'

'Ah . . .'

Olive's smile split her face. He saw where her teeth were missing. He looked down again at his tea mug.

'You mustn't tell,' he said obstinately. 'You mustn't talk to anyone about it.'

He was angry with himself for talking too much. What did he think he was doing, discussing her in front of Olive? She wasn't fit to breathe the same air, to walk on the same planet. He felt sour within, as if he had committed a sort of blasphemy.

'It's all right, love,' she said, leaning over the table to pat the back of his hand. He recoiled from her flabby touch. She spoke in a conspiratorial tone. 'I know about secrets, don't fret. My Philip and me, we're secret. I think we'll probably get married one day, but we're not in any rush. He doesn't tell anyone about me, not even in the interviews. I've got them all, you know, every one. Ever ever ever.'

She indicated one of the piles of papers that littered the table. Those at the bottom were yellowed and torn.

'I'm a bit behind with my filing, I'm afraid. I've got to get on with it: I promised him, and he'll be ever so upset if I don't get finished. He does like to look at his scrapbooks. We've got eleven, soon it'll be twelve. I'm his custodian, that's what he calls me, I'm like an archivist, you know? I've got fourteen videos, just of Philip. Did you see *Walter Raleigh*?'

'No.'

'He was ever so good. He always is. That was his big break, you know. I've got some fabulous early stuff, from before he was famous, that's why I got the satellite dish, to watch the old repeats. He was in *Softly, Softly*, and *Z Cars*, and *Callan*. He was a policeman in *Callan*, but not in the other two, which is funny, don't you think? I've even

got him doing one line in *The Persuaders*, with Tony Curtis
and Roger Moore. He looked just the same, he hasn't aged
a bit. Do you remember *The Persuaders*?'

'No.'

'It's a real treasure trove, my collection. It's like Alad-
din's cave, I'm going to donate it to a museum one day.
Did you see *Chapter and Verse*?'

'No.'

'Didn't you? They only showed it last month. Don't you
watch much telly?'

'No.'

'Well you can watch *Chapter and Verse* any time you
want. Or any of the videos. Just give me a call. I'll show
you my special souvenir, if you ask me nicely.'

Her smile had become coy. He returned it fleetingly,
then looked at his watch and seemed suddenly struck.

'I must go. Thanks for –'

'No, wait! Here's Sean. You must meet Sean. Cooee!'

She was waving energetically through the window. A
shadow fell through the glass as a big, burly figure in a
dark anorak passed by. A moment later they heard the
front door rattle open.

'Wipe your boots, dear!' Olive called out.

They heard the sound of boot soles scraping the doormat.

'We're in here,' said Olive needlessly.

Sean came into the kitchen. Not only did he have to
stoop, he practically had to squeeze in sideways. He was
huge.

'This is my son,' said Olive. 'Sean, this is Mr Forrester.
Jeffrey. Our new guest, remember? I told you all about
him. Say hello.'

Sean wiped his palms on his mud-stained jeans before
offering his hand. The guest accepted it reluctantly.
Besides being black with dirt the hand was gnarled and
callused, and the grip, when it closed, was hard enough
to make a strong man yelp. Jeffrey Forrester bit his lip and

tried a friendly smile. The look he got back was somewhere between guarded wariness and outright hostility.

'Sean, wash your hands!'

Sean went to the sink silently. Jeffrey Forrester nursed his crushed fingers under the table.

'Get yourself a mug, Sean. There's tea in the pot. And take off that jacket.'

Sean hung up his anorak on the back of the door and came over. He was wearing a red check shirt which, like his mother's clothes, seemed barely able to contain him, but in his case it was muscle, not fat, that extruded. He had Olive's exact pale eyes and lank sandy hair. It was like looking at two peas from a misshapen pod.

'Sean's been working hard all day. We keep the farm working together, you know. We're a team, he's the brawn and I'm the brains. Isn't that right, dear?'

Sean's answer was an almost imperceptible nod. Mother and son both stared fixedly at their guest. The combined focus of those four identical eyes seemed to bore right through him.

'I've got to be going,' he said uncomfortably, starting to rise. 'Thanks for –'

'Wait!' commanded Olive. 'You can't go yet. You wanted to see my souvenir, remember? Stay here, I won't be a moment. Sean will entertain you, won't you, Sean?'

Olive heaved herself up from the table and set off stiffly across the kitchen floor. At the door she glanced back over her shoulder.

'I'm expecting Philip tonight, Sean. If he comes while I'm upstairs you'll be sure to let him in, won't you?'

Sean went very still. A little colour drained from his ruddy cheeks. His mother's footsteps receded away down the hall and up the stairs, leaving an uneasy silence. After long and painful hesitation, he cleared his throat.

'Don't mind my mum. She's got some funny ideas in her head, but she doesn't mean harm.'

66

His voice was startlingly soft. It wasn't that he was trying to keep it down, out of his mother's hearing, it was just naturally light, high-pitched, almost girlish. He had a slight sibillant *s*.

'I know,' said Jeffrey Forrester, when he had overcome his surprise. He took a handkerchief from his pocket and blew his nose.

Speaking seemed to have released something in Sean. Words, and tension, poured out of him.

'She spends too much time on her own, you know? We both do, but it's worse for her, she doesn't get out much. She's got an active imagination, that's what the doctor says. Do you want more tea?'

'No thanks.'

'Beer?'

'Nothing, thanks.'

'Give me a shout if you change your mind.'

Sean gave a convivial smile. He had changed from blanket surliness to complete complaisance even with opening his mouth. He rocked back in his chair, spread his legs and crossed his arms in the pose of a genial host.

'How you finding the cottage then?'

'Fine, thanks.'

'It's good to have someone in it again. Been empty for over a year now. Warm enough for you, is it?'

'Yeah, thanks.'

'Only you seem a bit snuffly. Got a cold, have you?'

'I'm not sure. Bit blocked up.'

'Could be the rape. Though it's a bit early. Lots of town- ' ies get runny eyes and noses about now. You don't mind me calling you that, do you – townie?'

'No.'

'Where you from then? London?'

'Yeah.'

'That's what makes me sneeze, you know: the traffic, the exhaust. Is it a holiday or are you working down here?'

'Looking for work. I know what you mean about the traffic. Fancied a break myself. Stroke of luck I ran into your mum, at the theatre.'

'At the theatre, was it? She didn't say.'

'We were just queueing for autographs, you know. Didn't get any, none of the actors were there, so we just, like, got talking. She told me about the cottage.'

'What work you do?'

'Driving, mostly. Got my own van. It's outside, the white Astra.'

'Yeah, I saw it. Courier work?'

'Yeah. Last job was with a florist's, short-term contract; did that for a couple of months, working out of Hammersmith, delivering all over though. But I'll drive for anyone, you name it.'

'Your own boss, eh? That's how I like it too. My own man. Though sometimes I think –'

He stopped in mid-sentence. His mother was coming back down the stairs. She could be heard grunting and breathing heavily.

'Come on, you awkward bugger,' she said cheerily, out in the hall.

Sean was frowning hard at his hands. He seemed to be noticing the ingrained dirt for the first time. He got up and made for the sink, where he seized a nailbrush and set to work with intense concentration. His back was set firmly to the door.

'Here we are then,' said Olive coming in. 'Here's Philip.'

She was carrying a full-size cardboard cutout of her hero. It was crude and somewhat lopsided, evidently a home-made job. The body was painted black, with a fleshy dab at each side to indicate the hands. The head was a grainy blow-up photograph of Philip Fletcher in a clerical dog collar.

'From *Chapter and Verse*, you know,' explained Olive. 'Philip was the dean. That naughty, randy dean! I got the photo from the *TV Times*, had it enlarged. What do you think, Jeffrey?'

'Very nice,' he mumbled in reply. 'I really have to go now. Thanks for the tea.'

'Any time. And any time you want to see the videos, let me know. Say goodbye, Sean.'

Sean set to his scrubbing with redoubled energy. He said nothing.

'I'll see you out,' said Olive.

'Don't bother,' said her tenant hastily. 'I'll let myself out. Bye.'

He hurried out, anxious lest she think of another pretext to detain him. He half ran out of the door, and didn't slacken his pace even after he was through the gate. He stopped off momentarily at his van, snatched his shopping from the driver's seat, then carried on down the track to the cottage.

The track was no longer than fifty yards, but it curved sharply just before the end and so the cottage seemed quite hidden away, in a little dip behind a copse. From the outside it looked derelict, it was hardly surprising that there hadn't been a tenant for so long. Inside, it was bare but habitable.

He went in round the back, through the all-glass kitchen door. The kitchen was a modern extension, a flat-roofed oblong in sandy brick that didn't fit in with the weather-beaten wisteria-clad front. The rest of the ground floor had been knocked into one, a big but low-roofed sitting and dining room, sparsely furnished. There was a bathroom at the foot of the stairs, which led up to a landing and two bedrooms. He went immediately to the one at the back, which was the larger of the two.

It was cramped, nonetheless. A double bed took up most of the space, a wardrobe and a chest of drawers jostled for the rest. The blue floral wallpaper was old and peeling, the plaster ceiling cracked and patchy with damp. The other bedroom was no better, though he'd been thinking that he might try it out. He hadn't yet unpacked his suitcase.

69

He had brought with him only the bare necessities: a washbag and towel, a few shirts, underwear, a spare pair of trousers, his cassette recorder and his photograph albums. He needed to get some wellingtons. He usually only wore his trainers, he didn't have any other comfortable shoes, but he'd never lived in the country before, he'd never known about mud. He hadn't planned to take the cottage, it had been a spur-of-the-moment decision, though as soon as he'd made it he'd known he was doing the right thing. It took an hour and a half to get down to Chichester, so it was a three-hour round trip, and that was on a good day, without heavy traffic and roadworks. These days he was getting sick of driving. He'd spend ten, twelve hours a day in his van, depending on his workload. And he always had plenty on, he never turned down a job, no matter how tired he felt. He earned plenty and he didn't spend much, so he could afford to pay double rent, at least for the time being. He'd called the despatch firm where he was working and said he wanted some time off. They hadn't liked it, but they'd given him a few days with the promise of a full week at the end of the month. Till then he had the weekends.

He shoved his suitcase up to the head of the bed to make some room and took out his photograph albums. He had two, both new, identical ring binders with clear plastic sleeves on each page to protect the prints. He laid them side by side on the bed, resisting the temptation that welled overwhelmingly inside him to pore over them. He forced himself to be patient.

He emptied the contents of his white plastic shopping bag on to the bed. He had bought three new magazines. He would have bought more, there were so many to choose from, but he hadn't wanted to draw attention to himself; he hated the thought of people looking at him in the shop and thinking what a perve he was, sniggering at him. He had waited till there wasn't a queue, then given the exact change, thrust the magazines into the bottom of his bag and hurried out without catching the shopgirl's eye.

He opened one of the magazines, and thumbed impatiently through a few pages of text until he came to the first set of photographs. The model was blonde. He turned the pages quickly. The next girl was blonde too, and the one after her was Asian. The fourth girl was a brunette.

He examined the brunette's body critically. He wasn't interested in the face – he placed his hand over each photo in turn to block it off. It was quite a good body, though maybe a little plump. He didn't really like this magazine, he found the style too blatant, but a couple of pictures were all right. There was one where the girl was face down on a bed, naked except for her black stockings, looking back at the camera over her shoulder. The important thing was that the hair was short, so it didn't spill over the shoulders and back. He liked the pose. It was tasteful, not too revealing. He didn't like it when they left nothing to the imagination.

He took a large brown envelope from the back of one of the albums and carefully removed the contents. He was looking for one face in particular. It had come from a shot of her on her own, standing on a balcony somewhere with a very blue sky behind. It must have been on holiday somewhere, Greece or Spain. She had been leaning forward over the balcony rail, but looking back at the photographer.

He found it. Her beautiful dark eyes were smiling at him. His mouth was going dry, his pulse was quickening. He could feel that delicious, awful ache of longing building up inside him.

'Oh Sally,' he whispered to the photograph. 'Sally, my love, when will you be mine?'

There was still a little bit of that Mediterranean blue around her hair. He found his scissors and trimmed the photograph carefully. It fitted almost perfectly on to the body of the girl in the magazine.

He was feeling unbearably excited. He wanted desperately to cut out the new photograph and stick it into his album, to go through them all, to unleash his fantasies, to satisfy his desire. But it was much too early. It would be better later, at the end of the day, when he could dream her in bed with him. He would coax his fantasy to its exquisite climax, then go to sleep with her white nightdress pressed to his face, inhaling every last lingering drop of her scent. He would make himself wait. He was proud of his self-control.

He glanced through the other magazines briefly. There was one model who might have been suitable, but he stared accidentally at her face and felt revolted by her bright lipstick and coarse features. Her lips were parted, her heavy-lidded eyes invited his lust. He threw the magazine violently to the floor. He didn't want to taint himself with thinking of anyone else.

He took his cassette recorder from the suitcase and went downstairs. He sat down at one end of the dining table and stared hard, with half-closed eyes, at the chair opposite. He fancied he could see her face. He knew she was in the room with him. He checked that the microphone was connected, then pressed the record button.

'So, Sally, what do you think of our little love nest? Cosy, isn't it? We're hidden away safe, no one'll ever find us. I've got everything ready for you, my love. I got your favourite flowers. When are you coming, Sally? Don't keep me hanging round. Come soon.'

He pressed PAUSE. Her picture was slipping out of focus, his head was filled with thoughts that shouldn't be there. Some of the things Olive had said got under his skin. Her stupid fantasy about that actor annoyed him. The man wasn't ever going to come to her. Why did she go on about it? She was thinking the same thing he was thinking, but she had no reason. It wasn't the same at all, she had no right to think like that. He was angry. What he and Sally had was pure. This Philip person was nothing, nothing to Olive and nothing to anyone. He wouldn't be interested in that fat ugly slag Olive. He'd have his eye on other girls.

'I don't want anyone near you, Sally, you understand? You know I'm the jealous type, I told you so, I can't help myself, it's just the way I am. But I don't like these other men hanging round. You've got to give up this acting, I don't like to see you smooching with other men, even if it's only pretend. You should be here for me when I get home, me on my own, you shouldn't even need to talk to other men, not if you respect me. That's how I feel about you; I don't think about other women, so it's only fair, right? That Philip tries to chat you up, I'll kill him, so tell him to keep away, for his own good. And that goes for the rest. Any of them lays a finger on you, I'll do him, you hear?'

He paused the recorder again. He was so angry he could hardly get the words out. Sweat ran down his face, he was so tense he had to gasp for breath. Those pictures in his head of her with other men wouldn't go away. He remembered the photos as he'd found them in her flat, particularly those ones of a boating holiday: her in the stern with a thin blond boy, his arm round her, his hand on her bare waist, his lips daring to brush her hair. He'd cut him out of course, cut him with scissors, taken her and her alone for his album. But if that boy were here now, and he had those scissors in his hand, he'd stick him, and stick him, and stick him again till he squealed like a pig and the blood spurted like a fountain.

He could breathe easier now. The violent images calmed him, diffused his nervous energy. He got up and walked over to the window, hugging the recorder in his arms.

'Don't be upset by the blood, Sally, don't . . . I don't want you to have to look at these things, but I've got to protect you, look after you. You mustn't trust these bad men. Don't trust anyone but me. They don't want me around, they want to keep you for themselves, I know the way they think, but I'll find you, don't worry . . . soon . . . I saw you yesterday, driving off. By the time I got to the van you'd gone, but I'll find you, they can't keep you hidden much longer . . . we're . . . They won't like it when we elope, they won't, they . . . that's why they won't tell me where you are. You'd tell me, of course, but they won't let you and . . . it's a test, I've got to find you, and show I'm worthy, and I will. I will find you, Sally, I will . . .'

His voice was so choked he could hardly speak. He hated crying, he hated weakness, but he couldn't stop himself. It was so unfair, he couldn't bear it. He wanted her, and he knew she wanted him, so why weren't they together? He had to get word to her, to put her mind at rest, let her know that he was coming for her, that it was all going to be all right, that perfect happiness was just round the corner. He had to be careful, though. No one else must know that he was around. If they did they'd only try and stop him.

He dried his face, closed his eyes and clenched his body in concentration. He willed himself to be strong. It was nearly five o'clock, he couldn't afford to let precious time tick away. He checked that his keys were in his pocket. Everything he needed, his camera and binoculars, were in the van. He turned on the recorder, held the microphone very close to his lips, and whispered into it one last time:

'Not long now, my love. Be patient. You will be mine, Sally. Soon.'

It was a thought almost too exquisite to bear. He dropped the cassette recorder into a chair and bolted from the house, the wild fancies in his head carrying him almost skimming over the thick sticky mud.

7

As the weeks of rehearsal passed and the play began to take shape, so too did Sally's life. She hadn't told anyone in Chichester about the break-in. She carried it like a guilty secret, an unpleasant experience that would sooner be forgotten if never mentioned. Even Liz alluded to it only once during one of their regular long-distance phone calls, and that was in the context of telling her that Dave had approved the new locks on her bedroom window. Sally had moved the conversation on quickly to demand of what else had Dave expressed his approval, and it had soon degenerated, as it was wont to do, into ribaldry and teasing. Liz had remained stony, determined to give nothing away. Sally found her evasiveness as revealing as it was uncharacteristic.

The production was looking promising. Trevor may not have been the most inspiring of directors, but he was quietly competent and strict enough to keep a check on the kind of camp excesses which tend to surface inexorably in Restoration comedies. The acting was uniformly good, there were no weak links, and while there were frictions, the company as a whole was sufficiently professional to contain them. Sally still found Philip Fletcher rather cool and distant, but, as Dawn pointed out, she was hardly the first to voice that complaint. In any case, he brought such concentrated energy to the part that she found, to her private surprise, that she enjoyed her scenes with him the best.

Her days were filled by the play, the nights by text work and an unexpectedly intense ad hoc social life. It was a big company, and it divided naturally into groups along age lines. The older actors pretty much kept to themselves, though for different reasons. Neither Antonia Lynn nor Roy Power were seen much out of rehearsals, in Antonia's case because she was too frail, in Roy's because it meant he might have to buy somebody a drink. Everyone else congregated naturally in the pub most evenings. Some, such as Julian, tended to stay there until closing time. The youngsters, Sally amongst them, played tennis.

She had never in her life felt so fit. The inclemencies of an English spring notwithstanding, she played a set or two most evenings, and cooled down in Penny's swimming pool when she got home. On sunny mornings she took a brisk swim before going into work. The combination of strenuous activity and country air had her sleeping like a baby. There was no repeat of the insomnia that had blighted her last night in London. Though the occasional dark thought surprised her in unguarded moments, she was almost able to convince herself that it had all happened in another life.

The first few weekends were a problem. As soon as rehearsals finished on Saturday afternoon there was an exodus to London. She stayed behind and played the tourist, taking in the restoration work at Uppark, the Roman palace at Fishbourne and the Anglo-Saxon church at Bosham. She enjoyed her sightseeing jaunts but felt uncomfortable at the thought of not being able to go home. While the others were looking forward to getting the play on so that they could enjoy more time off, she was already dreading it.

Fortunately, on the third weekend the whole cast stayed in Chichester. Robert had scheduled his cricket match for the Sunday and everyone seemed determined to make it the social highlight of the season. Hampers were packed, Pimms and sparkling wine were purchased by the case, while the majority of the chosen eleven, few of whom had touched bat or ball in anger since school, scavenged amongst the local shops for appropriate attire. The results would not in every case have merited approval at Lords.

The Sunday turned out fine, with a hint of breeze but no prospect of match-threatening rain. Sally had arranged to go round to Jenny's place to help prepare sandwiches and they set off together, carrying a heavily loaded picnic basket between them, in good time for the eleven o'clock start. Jenny's digs were in North Street, a convenient five minutes both from the theatre and the cricket ground, which was bounded on two sides by a well-preserved stretch of the ancient Roman wall and lay as if in a divinely manicured hollow amid the backstreets of the town. Had it not been for the absence of rain, it might have been a perfect cameo of an English country setting.

They arrived just as Robert was losing the toss, a significant moment in national sporting history that was captured for posterity by a photographer from the local press. The captain of the opposing team, a pub side carefully selected for their probable amateurism and certain beer bellies, elected to bat first. Each innings was to consist of thirty overs, with a forty-five-minute break for lunch in between.

Robert, the two Stephens and Philip Fletcher were the *Country Wife* representatives. Dick Jones and two young actors carried the flag for the studio theatre. The other four places in the team were filled by Nigel, the resident lighting director, and three of the crew. Robert's attempts to set a field by the book quickly foundered on the realization that only a handful of his team understood that a square leg was not a medical condition. The fielders placed

77

themselves around the pitch at roughly equidistant intervals and more or less as they pleased.

'To open the bowling from the pavilion end in the inaugural Festival Theatre Charity Bowl,' announced Roy Power over a tinny temporary PA system, 'Equity's very own answer to Dennis Lillee, Mr Philip Fletcher.'

Isolated smatterings of applause greeted this announcement. The event had been trailed in the local press, and a sprinkling of fans added to friends and families of the teams had brought the crowd up to around a hundred. The bowl to which Roy referred had been sitting in the window of a nearby antique shop until the previous afternoon and looked suspiciously like a soap dish.

'Philip, who will be bowling right arm medium pace, will shortly be appearing as Horner in the main house,' intoned Roy portentously. 'Tickets are still available from the box office, at all prices.'

'Would you buy a used timeshare from that man?' drawled Dawn Allen, stretching herself out languorously on a tartan rug while extending her wine glass with apparent reluctance in the direction of Julian's freshly popped bottle of Moët.

'Ssh, darling!' said Julian. 'Whatever you do don't let him know he's not appreciated.'

The PA system had been a last-minute idea. Nobody was quite sure whose it had been, but almost everyone was claiming credit for the suggestion to install Roy behind the microphone. For practical reasons the equipment had been set up on the boundary opposite the pavilion, which just happened to be the spot where the rest of the company had elected to congregate. Roy's absence was keenly felt, and sincerely enjoyed.

'I'm surprised you're not out there, Julian,' said Sally, settling down on the grass between Jenny and Dawn.

'I'm team physio,' responded Julian. 'On hand to give them a rub down as and when. It's a filthy job, but somebody's got to do it. Do you think the referee's waving at me?'

'No,' said Sally. 'To the scorer. And he's called an umpire.'

'Oh. And what's he mean?'

'He's indicating that Philip has just bowled a no-ball.'

Philip's second delivery, which they watched with unbated breath, at least had the merit of legality, though it was scarcely more effective than the first. The umpire was soon waving at the scorer again.

'And what's that one mean?' demanded Julian.

'Four runs. A boundary.'

'Is that good or bad?'

'Bad. For us.'

'Then why's Dick Jones laughing his head off?'

The rest of the over proved less eventful than the beginning. Philip conceded a few more runs but it looked like he was beginning to find his line and length. That, at least, was the opinion of Roy in the commentary box.

'First it's all no-balls and then he's finding his length,' remarked Julian in a bemused tone. 'Do you think I'm missing something?'

'Mentally or metaphorically?' Dawn demanded, rolling on to her stomach and laying out the Sunday newspapers within easy reach. 'Should you feel any need to hone your physio skills, Julian, don't hesitate to give my shoulders a rub.'

'It's not very exciting, is it?' said Jenny, sounding a little guilty. 'Do you think it's going to hot up soon?'

'I shouldn't count on it,' answered Dawn, not looking up from her paper. 'I don't know about you, dear, I'm here strictly for the booze.'

But even Dawn was up on her feet and cheering a moment later when Robert Hammond clean bowled the opposing team captain with his first delivery. Julian, though he scarcely understood the import of what had

79

just occurred, flung his arms about her waist and led her giddily round the rug in an impromptu victory jig. Dawn demanded that he compensate her for his rude familiarity with an extravagant refill.

The new batsman nicked Robert's second ball straight to the only slip, a badly underdressed member of the stage crew who might well have taken a simple catch had he not been standing nonchalantly with his hands in his pockets chatting to the wicketkeeper. The batsman played with exaggerated defensive caution for the rest of the over.

'And that's a wicket maiden for the theatre,' said Roy Power in his most self-satisfied tone. 'Robert Hammond is also appearing in *The Country Wife*, which opens the week after next.'

'Perhaps putting Roy on wasn't such a good idea after all,' Julian noted sagely. 'Are we winning yet?'

'It's a bit early to tell,' said Sally. 'But we must be in with a shout if Robert carries on like that. He's got a lovely action.'

'Careful, dear. That's how rumours start.'

Unfortunately there was no other bowler to match Robert, so while he was able to keep the batsmen pinned down at one end, they were able to score freely at the other. At the close of the innings the batting side had scored 128 for 6, with four wickets to Robert, one to Philip and the other to a fortuitous run-out. Robert seemed pleased with the team's performance, and with the spectators'.

'Thanks for your support, we couldn't have done it without you,' he called happily as he led his players off. 'Anyone got a drink to spare?'

'Here,' said Sally, pouring him a glass of white wine. 'Come and join us. You've played before, haven't you?'

'A little,' said Robert, sitting down beside her.

'So are you feeling optimistic?'

'Quietly, yes. It doesn't do to be too noisy at cricket, it's not the point.'

'You were quite noisy when you were appealing for that lbw just now.'

'True. Should have had it too.'

'I'm not so sure. The batsman seemed well on his front foot to me.'

'Sounds like you should be playing for us, not watching.'

'You didn't ask.'

'You didn't volunteer.'

'Fair enough. I learned to play a bit when I was a kid. Had no choice, really. Funnily enough my brothers didn't want to play netball.'

They were just settling into an exchange of childhood reminiscences when Robert was called away by the press photographer to arrange the team picture. He spent the rest of the lunch break sorting out the batting order, a topic on which the majority of his players held fierce opinions. When at last the dust had settled, Roy Power sprang back smoothly into action.

'Opening for the theatre we have Philip Fletcher and Martin Graves. Martin will be appearing shortly in *Right or Wrong* at the Minerva. Tickets for *Right or Wrong* are available from the main theatre box office, as, of course, are tickets for *The Country Wife* – in which I myself will be appearing – and all the plays for the rest of the reason, which lasts until October. Full programme details can be obtained from the foyer.'

'I hope somebody's recording all this,' said Dawn. 'It could prove invaluable in the treatment of insomnia.'

Philip was taking strike, and after some elaborate crease-marking and field surveillance he was ready to face the first delivery, to which he offered a careful defensive stroke. He played out the rest of the over in similar style.

'Why doesn't Fletcher hit the bloody thing?' Dick Jones

was heard to grumble. He was padded up and obviously straining at the bit to get in.

He didn't have long to wait. A huge shout went up from the opposing team and its supporters as Martin was caught at mid-off without troubling the scorers.

'Oh dear, dear, dear!' said Dawn, without, however, sounding too concerned. 'All hands to the pumps now, boys.'

Robert, who had been umpiring along with Nigel, came running off the pitch ahead of Martin, who drew a brief but sympathetic round of applause from the spectators.

'I'm batting fourth,' Robert explained, sitting down on the grass to don his pads. 'Will someone take over the umpiring? Bit of a blow losing Martin so early on. Good luck, Dick!'

Dick was already striding out, flinging his bat around aggressively. He acknowledged Robert with a confident thumbs-up. The spectators were giving him an enthusiastic send-off.

'And Richard Jones is coming in to take up the gauntlet,' announced Roy with measured sonority. 'It'll be Jones and Fletcher together at the crease. A treat for theatre and cricket lovers everywhere.'

'At least he didn't mention the box office,' remarked Dawn.

'Tickets for both *The Country Wife* and *Right or Wrong* can of course be purchased from the box office.'

Robert looked up from his pads at Sally.

'They're not exactly rushing to the wicket, are they? Why don't you umpire?'

'Me?'

'Yes. It won't be for long, Philip or I will take over as soon as we're out. At least you know the rules.'

'Go on!' said Julian. 'Don't play hard to get.'

'Play as hard to get as you want, dear,' countered Dawn from the colour supplement end.

'It's entirely up to you,' said Robert. 'There's nothing at all at stake apart from the honour and the good name of the theatrical profession.'

'Well, I've always had a soft spot for hopeless causes . . .'

Sally's approach to the wicket, announced with some incredulity by Roy Power, generated by far the biggest cheer of the afternoon, though Dick Jones was convinced that the applause was for him. As she took up the umpire's position behind the stumps, the opposing team captain came over. She had made up her mind that she was going to say something very rude should he make a sexist objection to her presence.

'Sorry to bother you, Miss Blair,' he said respectfully, taking a notebook out of his back pocket, 'but I couldn't trouble you for your autograph, could I?'

'Middle and off please, Umpire,' said Dick Jones grandly, making a great show of taking his guard. Her autograph signed, Sally obliged.

'Two balls left in this over,' she announced.

'Thank you, my dear,' said Dick, making a little bow. 'How refreshing to see a pretty face at the other end. And I don't mean Fletcher.'

Sally lowered her arm and the bowler came lumbering in with considerable huffing and puffing. The ball pitched invitingly short of the off stump and Dick took an almighty thwack at it. He missed completely. Philip gave a contemptuous snort.

'Do not saw the air with your hands thus . . .'

The bowler took an extra long run-up for his next delivery, but to no noticeable effect. The ball bounced as gently as the last one, but this time Dick met it with the middle of his bat and sent it crashing into the cover boundary for an unstoppable four. He acknowledged the roar of the crowd with a clenched fist.

'Over,' said Sally, and went to take up a position at square leg.

'Put some elbow grease into it, Philip,' said Dick, walking out to the middle of the pitch. Philip stayed pointedly where he was.

'I wasn't aware you were in possession of a coaching badge, Dick. Is there no beginning to your talents?'

'Ha ha, Philip. You don't need a PhD to hit a bloody cricket ball.'

'Luck and amateurism always go hand in hand.'

'Don't you ever stop thinking of your career?'

'Ha ha, Dick.'

'Ha ha, Philip.'

Dick returned to his position. The bowler steamed in and Philip, a study in concentration, blocked the ball with a textbook straight bat.

'For God's sake!' Dick muttered overloudly. 'We'll be drawing our pensions before he gets off the mark.'

Philip's answer was to flick the next ball deftly off his pads and set off for an easy single.

'Yes!' screamed Dick, thumping his bat down on the crease and turning back for a second run.

'No!' Philip shouted back.

'Yes!'

'No!'

It was like a terrible pantomime double act. They were each yelling at the other incoherently as they crossed, Philip having set off belatedly and obviously against his better judgement for the second run. Fortunately for him the return throw was wildly inaccurate and he just scraped home.

'What are you making such a fuss about?' demanded Dick scornfully.

'It was my call!'

'No it wasn't!'

'Yes it was!'

'No it wasn't!'

'Look behind you!' chipped in Sally, perhaps injudiciously.

Both men shot her a filthy look. They carried on staring.

'Sorry,' she mumbled guiltily.

They were still staring at her. And then she noticed that the wicketkeeper was too, and so was the bowler, and the umpire, and all the other fielders she could see. She glanced uneasily at Dick and Philip in turn, both of whom were wearing blank, gawping expressions, and then she realized that they weren't actually looking at her at all, but at some point beyond her shoulder. She turned round slowly and saw that there was a naked woman walking towards her. She blinked.

It was a hot afternoon, and there was a bit of a shimmer on the grass, but the naked woman was no mirage. She was only a few yards away and proceeding at a stately, measured step towards the wicket, and she was wearing nothing at all save a pair of tortoiseshell-framed spectacles. She was carrying what looked like a tin biscuit box in front of her, though not in such a way as to afford even a modicum of concealment. In any case, she would have needed more than a biscuit box. Though she was only a little over five feet tall she appeared to be almost as wide. She looked like a giant pink jelly on the move.

There was absolute silence both on the pitch and amongst the spectators. The woman brushed past Sally, apparently oblivious to her, a half-smile fixed on her lips, a serene expression in her big pale eyes. She marched straight up to the wicket and stopped in front of Philip Fletcher, who shifted about uneasily on his feet, clearly not sure where to look. The woman spoke.

'Well, it seems like I've got your attention at last!'

She chuckled. She bent over, not without difficulty, and placed the biscuit box on the ground.

'I've made you a little something. Not that you deserve

85

it, you naughty boy. If you don't come round and see me soon I shan't be responsible for my actions!'

Still chuckling, she turned round and started to walk back the way she had come, in the direction of the gate. This time she appeared to notice Sally, and she winked, as if sharing a confidence. Sally smiled back automatically, but already the woman, who seemed both considerably older and slower than the average streaker, had ceased to pay her attention. Her eyes fixed on some distant point beyond the boundary, she glided away across the grass without the least sign of haste, apparently oblivious to the hundred or so pairs of eyes riveted to her wobbling buttocks. No one moved and no one spoke until, after a long, long minute, she had disappeared from view behind some trees.

'Open the box,' said Dick Jones.

'Take the money,' said Sally automatically.

Philip took off his batting gloves and prised open the tin cautiously, peering in as if expecting to find a booby trap.

'It appears to be a fruitcake,' he announced with relief.

'Can I have a bit?' asked the opposing wicketkeeper.

Philip handed him the tin. There was an impromptu break while the more peckish members of the fielding side came up to demand a slice. A knife thoughtfully left in the bottom of the tin greatly facilitated distribution.

'Is there something you're not telling us, Philip?' asked Dick Jones in a tone of what was, for him, rather subdued malice.

'I'm as much in the dark as you are,' Philip answered mildly, too shocked even to bicker. 'Never seen her before in my life.'

'You mean that wasn't your agent?'

Even Philip laughed. Nigel said he thought he'd seen her outside the stage door a couple of times, and one of the opposing team thought he knew who she was.

'Has a farm, I think,' he said. 'Out Goodwood way, I've delivered there. Unusual name. Mrs Vibash, or something.'

'Not Olive?'

'That rings a bell. Might be, yes. Olive Vibash.'

'You're definitely not telling us something,' said Dick.

'Well, you can tell us afterwards,' said Nigel authoritatively. 'I think we'd better finish this cricket match, don't you?'

The biscuit tin was removed and play resumed. But Philip did not appear to have recovered his concentration. He played and missed a couple of times, then took a streaky single to retain the strike. The first ball of the next over stayed low and sneaked under his bat to strike his back pad. The bowler leapt into the air screaming his appeal and Sally had no option but to give him out leg before wicket.

'Hard luck, old boy,' Dick called out gaily as Philip shouldered his bat. 'Better leave it to the experts, eh?'

Philip muttered something about a stump and Dick's anal sphincter. Roy's voice, strangely silent since the streaker interlude, came back on air in crackly commentary mode.

'A generous round of applause for a valiant effort from Philip Fletcher. And now, with the score standing at seven for two, much rests on the shoulders of the theatre captain, Robert Hammond. Cometh the hour, cometh the man. Let's hope he doesn't have to over-exert himself just one week before *The Country Wife* is due to open in the main house.'

'This commentary is brought to you courtesy of Mogadon,' explained Dawn, who was standing on the boundary with a fresh glass of sparkling wine to welcome Philip back. He took a grateful sip. 'Julian's guarding the remains of your cake. Apparently it's excellent. We're assuming that the lady was a strippagram and that it's your birthday. How very remiss of you not to let us know.'

'It isn't. And she wasn't. Did anybody see where she went?'

'Not really. Over there somewhere.'

'Please excuse me, I'm just going to have a look.'

'Are you sure that's wise?'

'Not entirely.'

'Well, if you find her, please bring her back. Her appearance livened up the match no end.'

Philip handed Dawn his glass and set off round the boundary. On the way he passed Roy, who wasn't sure but thought that he might have seen the woman go out to the road by the corner gate. Philip carried on in the direction indicated.

He wasn't quite sure what he was doing, or what he would say to the woman if he found her, but he was agitated and he felt a compulsion at least to be doing something. He was certain that the woman was Olive. He had the outsize knickers to prove it – like Cinderella with her slipper it seemed indubitable that the streaker and the lingerie would make a perfect combination. But what was her agenda? Her behaviour was bizarre, to say the least, but was it dangerous? Obsessed fans were usually only an irritation, but there was a fine line between obsession and mental imbalance. Writing letters was one thing, parading naked in public another. But might it not be a kind of practical joke, a dare? The whole business had a surreal air, as of an elaborate hoax. What if someone had put her up to it, just to make him overreact and look ridiculous – someone like Dick Jones?

Philip was aiming at the far corner of the ground, at a shady spot, dotted with trees, beyond which was a white iron gate. As he drew nearer he saw that there was a man kneeling beside one of the trees. The man, who was thickset and thirtyish, was dressed all in black, in T-shirt,

88

jeans and a baseball cap, and had a pair of binoculars round his neck and a camera with a telephoto lens in his hands. He seemed to be staring at Philip, though as he was wearing mirror sunglasses it was impossible to tell. Philip hailed him from a distance of about twenty yards.

'Excuse me, you haven't seen anybody come this way, have you?'

The man didn't answer. Instead he jumped to his feet in a startled manner, as if astonished at finding himself so addressed.

'I mean a woman,' continued Philip pleasantly, drawing nearer. 'Rather large; you couldn't miss her – she wasn't wearing any clothes. Just how I like them. Usually. Ha ha.'

The man paused for a moment, then took half a step towards Philip, who stopped where he was. The man jabbed a finger at him.

'I'm warning you! You keep your filthy hands to yourself!'

'I beg your pardon?' said Philip, not unnaturally taken aback.

The man in black said nothing more, but left his finger pointing the air in a threatening, warning gesture. And then, quite suddenly, he turned on his heels and sprinted for the gate, clutching his camera and binoculars to his chest. He carried on running down the road, where he raced out of sight round the nearest corner. A few moments later Philip heard the roar of an over-revved engine, and then a dirty white van shot briefly into view before disappearing again in an orgy of frictive rubber.

'Something I said?' Philip wondered aloud.

He walked out into the road and had a quick look about, but there was no sign of Olive or, indeed, of anyone. Clearly she had not lingered after delivering her cake. Philip walked back slowly towards the pavilion, where he arrived in time to see Robert Hammond strike the first six of the afternoon. Rather annoyingly, Dick Jones was still keeping him company.

'Find anything?' Dawn enquired on his return. Philip shook his head.

'Peculiar lot the people round here, aren't they? Do you suppose there's something in the water?'

'I wouldn't know. I never touch the stuff.'

As if to emphasize the point she held out her glass for Julian to refill. He obliged, but Philip declined to join in the demolition of yet another bottle on the grounds (entirely spurious as far as Dawn and Julian were concerned) that he wanted to keep a clear head for looking at his lines later tonight. About an hour afterwards, however, when Robert had hit the winning runs with his third and most majestic six, he did relent, and allowed himself to be swept along in the cork-popping alcoholic euphoria of victory.

8

After the cricket Sally and Jenny slipped away for a game of tennis, but Jenny had drunk rather more than either of them had realized and after only a few points the match had to be abandoned due to alcoholic excess. Jenny was shamefacedly apologetic, but Sally felt secretly relieved. They had an important run of the play the next morning, and she wasn't in the mood for exerting herself. Accordingly she refused Jenny's invitation to reconvene in the pub later and set off for home instead, feeling in no small measure dazzled at her own conscientiousness. Dick Jones wasn't back yet, and she guessed that Penny and her husband were also out. All the windows in the big house were closed, despite the heat of the day, and there were no cars in the driveway.

It was still warm, she felt sticky after being in the car, and the bright blue oval of the swimming pool looked more than usually inviting. She dumped her bag in the flat, grabbed her swimming costume on the run and raced down to the end of the garden.

The shock of the cold water was the most exhilarating sensation of the weekend. She swam a few lengths, then took a deep breath and sank down to the bottom of the deep end, feeling the sharp coldness tingling through her, re-energizing her tepid blood. She held her breath for as long as she could, surfaced to gulp in air, then sank back again into embryonic vein.

A faint dark flicker ran through the water above her, as of a shadow falling across the surface. She felt a pricking in the nape of her neck, an indefinable but potent sensation that she was being watched. She jerked her body round and looked up.

A face hovered over the edge of the water. The setting sun was behind it, she saw only a pale wavy blur, sensed but did not see the eyes staring at her. She steadied her feet against the bottom of the pool and kicked upwards.

It took only a second or two to reach the surface, but in that time the face had gone. There were thick shrubs and bushes round that side of the pool, and beyond a small orchard that ran all the way down to the fence at the boundary of the garden. She trod water gently and listened, but could hear nothing over her own heavy breathing.

'Hello? Anyone there?'

Her voice sounded thin and distant. Her ears were filled with water, she might as well still have been six feet under. She stared hard at the bushes. There seemed to be movement, but it might have been a bird, or the wind. She arched her body suddenly and swam backwards to the shallow end, keeping her eye on the bushes.

She hauled herself out and sat on the edge of the pool, her feet in the water. The bushes moved again, but this time it was definitely wind, a chilly gust that clawed her bare shoulders and set her shivering. The sun was now hidden by clouds and the temperature had dropped. She looked round for her towel.

'Hello there,' said a voice from somewhere close behind.

She gave an involuntary yelp as she jumped back into the pool. She splashed around like a startled duck.

'I'm sorry,' chuckled Dick Jones. 'Did I surprise you?'

Only the coldness of the water saved her blushes. Dick Jones seemed amused.

'Sorry, creeping over the grass like that. I should have shouted out. Here, let me give you a hand.'

She had started to pull herself out of the pool again. He took hold of her under the armpits and helped her to her feet.

'Cold!' he exclaimed, almost as an admonishment, giving her shoulders a brisk rub. He reached down for her towel. Sally's nostrils were infiltrated by a pungent combination of sweat and aftershave. Dick was still in his cricketing whites.

'Thanks,' she murmured, taking the towel and enfolding herself in it. She glanced back towards the bushes. 'Have you been back long?'

'No. Just got in. You didn't hear my car, obviously.'

She hadn't, but she saw it now, an overtly phallic streak of red aggressively nudging the tail of her demure little Citroën.

'I was underwater,' she explained. 'I'm sure I saw someone, by the deep end. That wasn't you, was it?'

'No. I don't think there is anyone about, is there? Unless it was the gardener.'

'Not on a Sunday.'

She knew she'd seen something, she didn't think for a second that she might have imagined it. The very indistinctness of that face was haunting. Her gaze remained fixed on the bushes.

'Excuse me a moment,' she said, walking round quickly to the far end of the pool. The rhododendrons were in full bloom, the bushes were thick and lush. There were some narrow gaps, but, lacking as she did native tracking skills, there was no way of ascertaining whether anyone had passed through one of them recently. In any case, whoever it was had had ample opportunity to slip away.

'No one there now,' said Dick Jones, echoing her thoughts. 'It was probably a kid, from next door. Shouldn't you put some clothes on? It's getting nippy.'

It was. The wind was up again and the evening sun was now thoroughly immured within a dense blanket of cloud. Dick came towards her, offering his sweater.

'No thanks,' she said. 'It'll only get wet. I'll pop back in and dry off.'

'Then the least you can let me do is pour you a Scotch. Come down as soon as you're dressed.'

'Thanks, that would be lovely. I'll see you in a minute.'

A Scotch was just what she'd been yearning for, and she didn't have any. She was feeling a little uneasy too, and would be glad of the company. She sprinted back to her flat, took a brief shower, then dried and dressed and went downstairs. Dick's door was open and he called out for her to come in.

She hadn't been inside his flat before, though not for lack of invitations. It was almost automatic for him, whenever their paths crossed in the Green Room or at the stage door, to ask her to drop in some time, any time, but all she wanted to do when she got back in the evening was to grab a quick bite and study her next day's lines before going to bed. Thus far during this job, and probably for the first time in her career, she had been an object lesson in sobriety and dedicated single-mindedness. Dick, by contrast, was a serious roisterer, who tended to regard last orders in the pub as a comma, not a full stop, and would therefore usually be beginning his serious night's work just as she was preparing for sleep. It was as well that the floor between them was solid. Even as it was she usually drifted off to the accompaniment of his aggressively nostalgic taste in music.

He was on the phone when she came in, dressed in a green silk dressing gown and showing off a deal of hairy thigh. His thick black hair was wet and he'd obviously just come out of the shower himself. Sally sat on a chair by the door and admired the spacious interior, which boasted roughly the dimensions of a squash court. The ceiling was up at about two-thirds the height of the building; her own flat above, she supposed, must have once been the hayloft. A spiral staircase opposite led up to a deep gallery containing a curtained bed. Doors either side of the base indicated

94

the kitchen and bathroom. The furnishings had a solid traditional feel. The subtle lighting came from spotlights attached discreetly to the oaken wall beams.

'Eight o'clock then, Jean-Paul?' said Dick into the phone. 'Good.'

He put down the receiver and turned to a drinks cabinet in the corner.

'Ice in your Scotch?'

'No thanks. But could I have a little water?'

'Only a little. It doesn't do to dilute the taste of Glenlivet.'

As if to emphasize the truth of this proposition he poured himself the equivalent of a neat treble. He handed Sally her glass.

'Cheers.'

'Thanks, Dick.'

'I hope you haven't eaten. I've taken the liberty of booking a table.'

'Oh.'

Liberty seemed a bit of an understatement.

'Come on!' he said cajolingly. 'We have a victory to celebrate!'

She hesitated. She had come back for some quiet study and an early night, but now she was feeling a little nervous at the prospect of spending the evening alone. Though reason told her that her experience at the pool was probably innocent (as Dick suggested, a nosy kid was the likeliest explanation), nonetheless that glimpsed blurred face continued to nudge at her imagination. Her subconscious was so full of barely suppressed nightmares that it didn't take much to stir them up.

'Well, all right, Dick, but I mustn't be late.'

'Nor me, we've got a big day tomorrow. But it was a pretty big day today and I don't think we should let it pass without due commemoration. My own contribution may have been, on the surface, modest, but it's a team game, as Robert kept telling us, and though he was the star (let's not deny credit where it's due) I don't think he could have done it without me.'

'No.'

'I was the rock on which the innings was built. Robert said I was an anchor.'

She wondered if he had heard him correctly.

'Of course, I'm more of a rugby man myself, as you'd expect. Pretty useful scrum half, though I say so myself. I was about to have a trial for Welsh Schoolboys when I did my knee in. Who knows what might have been, eh? You follow rugby at all?'

'No.'

It didn't stop him talking about it. He offered her a history and commentary on the state of recent Welsh rugby; a comparison between Twickenham and the Cardiff Arms Park, touching briefly on contrasting architectural styles but focusing mainly on an appreciation of atmosphere, with the verdict, unsurprisingly, coming down in favour of Cardiff; and finally an assessment of each country's chances in the next Five Nations Championship.

'I'm not boring you, I hope?' he said sweetly, after predicting that Wales were likely to recapture the Triple Crown.

'Er, no.'

'I thought not. You look like a girl who appreciates the finer things in life. I can't stand actors who just talk shop, can you? It's five to eight, we'd better be off.'

'Where are we going?'

'Ah ha! My surprise – and my treat. If you'll excuse me a moment.'

He went through one of the doors by the spiral staircase into the bathroom. She could tell it was the bathroom because he left the door half open. Being a well brought up girl she looked away, but felt herself compelled to glance in a few moments later when she heard Dick making aggressive grunting noises. He had slipped out of his dressing gown and was wearing only a pair of white briefs. He appeared to be doing press-ups. After he had done about a half-dozen he sprang to his feet and set about combing his hair in the mirror. Sally got up and went over to inspect an uninteresting oil painting. Dick was humming 'Men of Harlech' slightly off-key. He was still humming it, and she was still looking at dull pictures, when at length he emerged, dressed in tan trousers and a yellow silk collarless shirt, and more thoroughly perfumed and combed than a Crufts champion.

'Your carriage awaits,' he announced with a little bow.

He escorted her outside to his red BMW and gallantly opened the passenger door.

'Better get that seat belt on,' he advised. 'She goes like a rocket.'

'Yes. I remember.'

'Of course. Ten past eight. I'd better step on it.'

They shot off down the driveway with the sounds of screeching tyres and crunching gravel reverberating in their ears. Dick turned off in the direction of Midhurst.

'Doesn't she handle beautifully?' he asked rhetorically. 'Not sure yet whether I'd put her ahead of the Merc. Traded in the Merc last year; she was a stunner, a real thoroughbred, but, as I say, I don't think I'd put a cigarette paper between them. Love them both equally, but in some ways I still hanker after my old Jag. You a car person at all?'

'Not really, no.'

He told her about his ex-Jaguar nonetheless, and about his ex-Mercedes too. He was sure that she would agree with him that the fuel-injected engine was the finest invention since Jane Russell's bra.

'I don't really know,' she shouted back over the roar of the engine.

'Just like a woman! The only thing that interests you about a car is the colour, eh? This is our turning.'

Sally was nearly impaled on the handbrake as Dick spun

97

the car aggressively through ninety degrees and raced off up a narrow lane. A meandering elderly cyclist was practically propelled from his saddle by the slipstream. Sally discreetly closed her eyes. Dick talked about four-wheel drive Porsches.

After a couple of miles the car slowed down. Sally dared to open her eyes again and saw that they were coming up to a pretty white-walled old mill house beside a small weir and a picturesque bridge. A board on the side of the house, trimmed in French national colours, announced it as LE SPECTRE DE LA ROSE. As he parked the car Dick informed her confidentially that it was the best Frog cooking this side of Calais.

'*Voilà!*' he declared at the door to the restaurant, indicating for her to go in. With seeming perversity he was now wearing a pair of very dark sunglasses.

Sally stepped inside. The theme of the restaurant was comical-pastoral, as exemplified by rustic implements in the decoration and caricature Gallic theatricality in the waitering. A droopy-eyed peasant with a thin moustache and otiose hand gestures came gliding across the rough stone floor.

'Ah, Meester Jones! What a pleasure to see you again!'

'*Ah non, Gaston, c'est tout mon plaisir.*' Dick boomed back regally. He noticed that some of the diners who had turned round in their seats at the sound of his voice couldn't see him properly, so he stepped further into the room to give them a better view. He looped a casual arm round Sally's shoulder. '*Et c'est encore mon plaisir pour à toi presenter ma chère jeune amie, la belle célèbre actrice et étoile de la futur, Mademoiselle Sally Blair.*'

'Mees Blair!' Gaston declaimed effusively, as to a long-lost friend. He bent to kiss her hand. 'I am charmed and delighted to meet you.'

Sally wondered if he was speaking English in the hope

of deterring Dick Jones from speaking French. If so, he wasn't succeeding.

'*Tu as preparé mon table normale, Gaston?*'

'Ah yes, Meester Jones, please follow me to your . . . usual table.'

The walls were lined with discreetly compartmented alcoves, and it was to one of these that Sally presumed Gaston was leading them. She was a little surprised, then, when he stopped suddenly in the exact middle of the restaurant and pulled out a chair for her at the most conspicuously non-discreet table. A number of waiters and kitchen staff, all originating, like Gaston, from Central Gallic Casting, came out to offer Dick obeisance. He accepted and returned their salutations generously. At length the extras all departed, Gaston having left them copies of the impressively thick menu and even denser wine list.

'The menu here is simply incomparable,' said Dick, adding, for greater effect: '*Simplement incomparable.*' He was holding it at an angle, trying to catch the light. 'When, of course, you can actually see to read it . . .'

'You could take off your sunglasses,' Sally suggested.

Dick laughed indulgently.

'One doesn't want to be recognized everywhere, my dear. We in the public eye need to have a little privacy from time to time.'

His need, alas, was for a time to remain unfulfilled. Barely had he ordered the aperitifs when the first of their fellow diners, a charmingly awkward middle-aged lady with a small child in tow, came across to beg for his autograph. By the time Gaston had departed with their full order, she had been followed by three others. Dick had fulfilled the obligations of stardom with perfect good grace. When at last they were left alone again he leant across the table and whispered to Sally in confidential tones.

'You must get this from time to time yourself, I expect. As soon as you've been on the telly they all seem to think they own you. Still, I think it's our duty, don't you, to bring a little ray of sunshine into their lives, whenever possible?'

'That's a very magnanimous sentiment, Dick.'

'*Noblesse oblige*, my dear. *Noblesse oblige*.'

She had been hoping that he wasn't going to say that.

'So,' he said, when he had duly tasted the dusty bottle of white Burgundy which Gaston had fetched expressly from the cellar, and pronounced it *simplement incomparable*, 'How are rehearsals going?'

'Oh, quite well, I think.'

'So are ours. You know how it is at the beginning, when you're stumbling around with a book in your hand, constantly stop-starting, you always think it'll never work, but then there comes that magical moment – it happened to us last Wednesday morning – when the sun seems suddenly to break through the clouds and you can see your way to the summit. You don't feel like a mere actor then, you feel like an explorer, an adventurer on the edge of discovery. Perhaps it's rash of me, but I'm modestly confident that we've got a potential monster success on our hands.'

'You think so?'

He did, and over the first course he told her at length why he did. By the time he had finished, Sally's eyes were as glazed as the onion and celeriac tart she had just consumed.

'Some interesting casting in your production,' observed Dick with a somewhat sly air as the waiter was clearing away their plates. 'It'll be fascinating to see how Philip copes with the demands of playing a juve lead in a long run.'

Sally had been wondering how long it would take him to bring up this topic.

'How were your mussels?' she asked. 'The onion tart was superb.'

'*Superbe, chérie, superbe* . . . which is more, I suspect, than

100

we're going to be able to say about Philip's performance.'

Sally began playing uncomfortably with her cutlery. Though she felt no personal loyalty to Philip, she felt a great deal for the production.

'He's actually very good,' she told Dick quietly.

'Oh, I'm sure he is. In a technical way. Don't get me wrong, I have the greatest respect for Philip. The greatest respect . . .'

She wondered what he usually said about people for whom he had the least respect.

'. . . It's just that Philip is hardly my idea of, shall we say . . .' with one hand he was gesturing as if groping for the right word; with the other he was stroking a thick clump of his chest hair '. . . well, he's not exactly my idea of a virile, sexually charismatic, magnetic leading man.'

Sally wondered just which actor in Chichester that season might have fulfilled his description.

'Do you know what Philip's fundamental problem is?'

She didn't, but she didn't expect to remain ignorant for long.

'He's too damned English, that's what it comes down to.'

'Well, if being English is the problem, I'm afraid that leaves quite a lot of us in the same boat.'

'No, no, I'm not talking about you. You're quite different, I can tell that. There's no fire in Philip, no passion, no spontaneity. He's just never lived. You've only got to look at him to know that. He's terminally buttoned up. He suffers from anaemia of the soul. It comes of having life too easy, I suspect. He's never known poverty, struggle, the grim reality of a life eked out at the coalface. I'm speaking metaphorically, you understand. I didn't have to face that life myself; my father sweated and strained every fibre of his being to ensure that I should never have to choke my lungs in the bowels of the earth to earn my bread. But the coal is in my blood. One does not forget easily that which cannot be forgotten.'

'I don't suppose one does,' said Sally, not because she had anything to say on the subject, but to remind him that she was still there. It didn't, alas, have much effect. Dick's eyes, focused on a faraway point somewhere between her left ear and the window, had misted over as soon as he began his lyrical wander down the sepiaed byways of memory lane. Not even the arrival of Gaston with a bottle even dustier than the first could interrupt the flow, though it may have contributed over the evening to a certain slurring in his speech. He seemed largely oblivious to Sally throughout the main course, at which he picked only fitfully. Sally wiped her own plate quite clean. She had little else to do.

'I'm sorry, going on about myself like this,' he said to her at last, when he noticed that she had finished her food. 'I'm not boring you, I hope.'

'No, of course not,' she said sweetly, deploying part of her own formidable battery of acting skills. Dick noticed that their glasses were empty.

'*Une autre bouteille, Gaston!*' he demanded, waving the old one over his head like a football rattle. He rested his forearms on the table and leant in towards her, oozing instant charm and solicitude. 'That's enough about me, let's talk about you. How come our paths have never crossed before?'

'Well, I, er, don't know.'

'Philip doesn't deserve you. He's always been lucky in his co-star, his own shortcomings are less apparent. Quite what the critics see in him I've never known. His whole career's a complete mystery, if you ask me.'

'I don't think you're being entirely fair, Dick.'

'Oh, don't get me wrong. I have the greatest respect for Philip, the greatest respect. To have got as far as he has with such limited resources is entirely commendable, I'm

102

the first to take my hat off to him. But he doesn't know his own limitations. He overreaches himself.'

'*Il a des idées au-dessus de sa gare?*' suggested Sally.

'Yes. You know his primary problem, of course?'

His pause took her by surprise. She wasn't used to him waiting for an answer to his questions.

'Er, his Englishness, isn't it?'

'No, no, besides that. His other primary problem.'

'And what's that?'

'Jealousy.'

He leant back and folded his arms with a sigh.

'Pure jealousy, my dear. It saddens me to say it. It pains me utterly to the core of my being. But there it is. The green-eyed monster. I'm reluctant, of course, to mention it. I only do so because I feel (and have done since the first moment of meeting you) such a special bond of trust between us, as between one professional and another, and I know how you of all people will appreciate that I'm speaking purely objectively in the spirit of truth and honesty and not out of (God forbid) personal spite or anything petty and malicious like that – you don't know me yet, it's true, but when you do you'll realize that none of that's in my nature. It's difficult, of course, because it sounds big-headed to speak of another's envy, but I can't deny what's plain before my face. It goes without saying that I bear no personal malice to Philip. To be frank, I've always felt rather sorry for him, and it's for that reason that I don't allow myself to resent his jealousy, though it would be scarcely unreasonable of me to deplore his small-mindedness. But I can afford to be generous. We should not sink to the level of those less fortunate than ourselves. Do you not agree?'

'The tarte au citron sounds inviting, doesn't it?' said Sally, who had been peering with absolute concentration at the dessert menu.

'You see, I'm coming more and more to the conclusion,

the more time I spend plying my modest trade in this extraordinary and in so many ways magical, great profession of ours, that the dividing line between actors of the first rank and the rest lies in the capacity to take risks. And that of course is where poor, dear Philip is forever doomed to remain earthbound. Like a dodo.'

'A dodo?'

'A flightless bird. An actor who cannot let his heart go and soar heavenwards is like a bird without wings. Like a eunuch in the arms of a siren. Like a Ferrari without a top gear. You follow? I'm sorry, I get carried away, inebriated with language. I drink and breathe this alien silver tongue of Avon's Swan. Though I am a Celt I can do no other. We each have our cross to bear.'

'Perhaps I'll just have a coffee,' Sally suggested to herself. Dick was pouring for himself the last of the second bottle of red wine.

'You know he's obsessed with me. Can't stop talking about me, venting his spleen – I have it on excellent authority. It's sad really, I don't give him a second thought, to me he's as inconsequential as a fly is to an elephant, but he just can't seem to get me out of his head.'

'I think I'll have an espresso.'

'We fell out over a woman, but that was a long time ago (she chose me, incidentally), it's only a pretext and he knows damned well it is. He just can't handle my success. I've had to struggle, I've come up the hard way. No silver spoons where I come from, only coal dust. You know Philip's biggest problem?'

'Jealousy?'

'No, he's English. Too damned English. Never done anything in his life, never stepped across the line, never dared, always used a safety net. But an actor has to be out there on the edge. There should be signs up outside every theatre: Danger! Actor at work! How can you be the repository of mankind's dreams and aspirations if you've

104

never done anything with your miserable, squalid, sub-urban life? The fact that he's got me under his skin is his problem, not mine, you know I never give him a second thought. It's pathetic, and you want to know another thing?'

'Ah, here comes the waiter. Shall we make that two coffees, Dick?'

'Fuck the coffee, I've got a bottle of Otard '37 back at the ranch. *Garçon!*'

He barely glanced at the bill before showering notes from a bulging wallet on to the table. With the effusive thanks of the waiters ringing in his ears he headed for the exit in a more or less straight line. Sally caught up with him at the door.

'Are you sure you're all right to drive, Dick?'

Dick gave a disbelieving snort.

'It takes more than a few bottles of *vin ordinaire* to knock me off my perch, honey. Where I come from men are men. And women are women.'

'How reassuringly traditional,' Sally murmured. She smiled uncertainly. Dick was staring at her with passionate intensity.

'Has anyone ever told you you're a devastatingly attractive young woman!' he demanded thickly.

'Oh *there's* the car!' exclaimed Sally happily, as if clapping eyes on a long-lost treasure. She headed swiftly for the red BMW, which was parked on the edge of the restaurant forecourt, in front of a dirty white van. Dick followed, at his own pace, and got in beside her. He appeared to be having difficulty fitting the key into the ignition. At length he succeeded, but he didn't start the engine. Instead he turned towards Sally, casually extending his left arm over the top of her seat.

'How come a beautiful woman like you is unattached?'

She wasn't aware that she'd told him she was. Perhaps he'd checked up on her, or maybe he was only drawing an obvious conclusion. At any rate it seemed pointless to issue a denial.

'Oh, I don't know,' she said lamely. 'Just one of those things!'

'I know,' he said huskily. 'It's so difficult in our business, we are gypsies forever in search of new paths to travel. Not for us the safe comforts of domestic bliss; there are always new worlds to conquer, new hearts to seduce, new passions to ignite. You're a kindred soul, Sally Blair, I knew it the moment I clapped eyes on you.'

'Did you?' She looked at her watch. 'Good God! Is that the time?'

'Time waits for no man, Sally Blair,' intoned Dick with solemn enigmatic irrelevance.

He struck like a viper. One moment he was sitting in his own seat, the next he was half in hers, the weight of his body jamming her against the upholstery, his left hand pinning her shoulders down. His other hand was up her skirt and his tongue was forcing its way between her lips. She tried to wriggle free but it was hopeless. She felt as if she were being smothered by a rampant bear.

Suddenly the car shook and jerked forward. A bright white light flashed across the windscreen. Dick snapped his head back furiously.

'What the bloody hell . . .'

The bright light was coming from the headlamps of the van immediately behind. The BMW had been shunted forward a good foot or more. The two vehicles were still bumper to bumper.

'Bastard!' screamed Dick, flinging open his door and staggering out. 'That's my bloody car, you bastard!'

Sally pulled herself round in her seat, struggling to recover her breath. She saw the van door open and the driver get out. Even with the light spilling from the headlamps and the restaurant his face was only a blur. Dick was squaring up to him, shaking his fist.

'You clumsy stupid idiot! If you've even so much as scratched that bumper I'll sue your bloody –'

Dick didn't finish the sentence. The dark shape of the van driver moved suddenly and Sally heard a sharp smacking noise. Dick crumpled to his knees. The van driver kicked him in the face.

Sally scrambled out of the car. The van driver was still kicking Dick, who was an inert lump on the concrete forecourt. Sally saw the white smudge of his assailant's face, turned in her direction. For the second time that day she experienced the strange sensation of unseen eyes boring through her.

She screamed. She was shocked, and she was terrified, but she had her wits about her. It was a warning scream, a lung-bursting yell for help, not a shriek of fear. She'd always had good projection. The van driver hesitated then took a step towards her. She turned and ran back towards the restaurant, where faces were pressed to every window. Gaston appeared in the doorway, a gaggle of waiters and customers squeezing up behind him in a bottleneck. She stumbled into their arms.

When she looked back the van had gone. One of the waiters was running off down the road after it, quite use-lessly – only the faint receding roar of the engine remained. Gaston and the others were attending Dick. Between them they hauled up his dead weight and carried him back towards the restaurant, his head lolling lifelessly and his feet trailing the ground. Blood streamed from his mouth and nose.

'He's dead!' one of the diners who had come to the door shouted disbelievingly. 'By God, he's dead!'

'Call an ambulance!' another shouted. 'Call the police!'

But someone already had. Barely had the noise of the retreating van melted away than the night air was filled with sirens.

9

'Rough or smooth?'

Long red-nailed fingers were poised to spin the racket on the red clay court. Philip didn't hesitate.

'Smooth.'

'Of course.'

Jennifer Armitage laughed as she released her grip on the handle. They watched it settle after a few token elliptical revolutions rough side up.

'I'll serve,' she pronounced, neatly flipping up a new yellow ball between her racket and her heel and catching it between finger and thumb. Philip watched admiringly as she walked sinuously back to the baseline. Her white micro skirt and the low cutaway top that exposed her midriff left him with plenty to admire.

'I expect you're glad you don't have a car,' she called back over her shoulder.

The shift in her train of thought might have baffled him at any time, but with his attention wholly absorbed by the gentle sway of her hips he didn't have a chance. When she turned back to face him he could only return her gaze blankly.

'I mean in view of events last night,' she explained. 'At least you can't be a victim of road rage.'

'Ah yes,' he said, swallowing the irritation that welled convulsively inside him. 'There is that.'

There was that, but not much else. He'd been suffering

all day from Dick Jones overload, a condition normally brought on by mere mention of the name but in the present instance exacerbated beyond all human bearing by media saturation. When Dawn had rung the previous night to tell him that Dick had been set upon and hospitalized by an irate motorist he had been barely able to contain his laughter, although he had made a very convincing stab at sounding concerned. But since the morning he had acquired an altogether more fitting sense of outrage. Jones had made the front page of almost every national newspaper. He had been on every TV news bulletin, and that afternoon there had even been a question in Parliament, followed by an expression of sympathy from a minister at the Home Office. Everyone had spoken of their shock and disgust at an assault on, to quote the witless, brain-dead MP, 'one of our best-loved and most distinguished actors'. The sympathy for Jones, propped up in his hospital bed with the entire national media hanging on his recovery, was overwhelming. Philip was utterly disgusted.

'Wasn't it ghastly?' said Jennifer, taking up her position ready to serve.

'Totally,' replied Philip with feeling.

'You're not safe anywhere these days, are you? Ready?'

He nodded. She tossed the ball up and threw her whole weight behind the racket. The ball skimmed over the net, bounced once an inch inside the line and flew with a dull thud into the wire fence at the back of the court. Philip hadn't moved.

'I'm sorry,' said Jennifer. 'Are you sure you were ready?'

'Er, yes,' answered Philip, as he began crossing to the other side of the court. 'It'll take me a few shots to get my eye in, I expect.'

'Fifteen-love then,' said Jennifer, and served again.

This time Philip managed to get his racket to the ball,

but the vicious topspin almost knocked it from his grasp.

'Thirty-love,' said Jennifer. 'It's lucky he had his girl-friend with him, isn't it? If she hadn't screamed for help he might have been killed.'

Philip connected with the next serve venomously. The ball crashed into the net.

'Bad luck,' said Jennifer. 'Forty-love. She's in your play, isn't she? Pretty girl.'

'Yes,' he answered tersely. There had been pictures of Sally in every paper as well. In the tabloids her photos had been bigger than Dick's, which was hardly surprising as she was a great deal more photogenic. She hadn't made any statement to the press, but there were sickening inter-views with waiters and restaurant customers who were all of the opinion that Dick and Sally had made a lovely couple. 'So much in love. You could tell by the way they gazed into each other's eyes,' some slimeball called Gaston was widely quoted as saying. Philip had practically vom-ited into his cornflakes. The morning's run of the play had been totally ruined, of course, with photographers poking their lenses through the rehearsal room window at every opportunity. He'd been thrown off his stride almost as much as Sally. Press interest showed no sign of abating. Today's London *Evening Standard* had really gone to town, with a feature reporting at length on why girls in their twenties found fortysomething men so attractive. Four out of five young women stopped and interviewed at ran-dom in the West End thought Dick Jones would be the ideal older mate. One said that he was the most fanciable man on TV. Philip wondered how recently she'd visited an optician.

'Game,' said Jennifer, as the ball flew past Philip's shoul-der without troubling his racket. He hadn't really been paying attention.

'Still getting my eye in,' he said lamely as they came to the net on their way to swapping ends.

'Yes, you said you were a bit rusty,' she said, laughing gaily. 'Never mind.'

He took up position and knocked in what he thought was a pretty good serve. Jennifer returned it effortlessly.

'Love-fifteen.'

He tried again.

'Love-thirty.'

Two serve and returns later and the game was over. He hadn't scored a point.

'You've done this before,' he said, forcing a smile.

'Played for the county before I got married,' she replied casually.

'Now she tells me!' exclaimed Philip, appealing for sympathy with a heavenwards glance.

He was at best an occasional social player and he was unused to having to raise his game above the level of bare competence. The women he normally played against tended to pat the ball with inoffensive ladylike delicacy, not launch it at him like a ballistic missile. She had warned him that she always played to win; it was the possibility of her playing to maim that bothered him.

She actually slipped up during the third game, missing two first serves in a row and giving him a decent sight of the ball. However, from love-thirty she powered her way smoothly to game without undue trouble. They took a break before the next game, pausing at the net to sip cold mineral water.

'You seem to be finding your rhythm,' said Jennifer.

'Perhaps,' said Philip warily. It being pretty obvious which way the wind was blowing, he thought he'd better get his excuses in now. 'I'm not fully mobile yet, I'm afraid. Cracked some ribs a while back, still recovering.'

It was true that he'd felt the odd intercostal twinge during the cricket match on Sunday, though it had hardly been debilitating. But he smiled at her with easy charm;

he was a natural born liar, greatly improved by dedicated training.

'Oh dear. You will be fit for your opening night, I hope. When is it?'

'Friday.'

Or four days' time, to look at it another way. The shadow play of rehearsals was over, exposure and performance beckoned, the die was cast. Tomorrow would be a technical day, Wednesday reserved for more teccing and the dress rehearsal. What they had now was, more or less, what the first preview audience would get on Thursday and the press twenty-four hours later, a prospect to disturb even the most sanguine temperament. And Philip's was a bilious mood.

After the morning's run they had been given the rest of the day off, Trevor amply enhancing his reputation as a hands-off director. Philip had taken the opportunity to shoot off back to London, a tedious round trip which he had completed just in time to respond to Jennifer's invitation to tennis. He had undertaken the dull journey home on account of Olive.

'Well I'm sure it'll be a great success,' said Jennifer. 'I can't wait.'

'You're coming to the first night?'

'Maybe, if I can find an escort. My husband won't be back.'

'He's going away, is he?'

'Gone already. Left this morning. For the Gulf. Be away for a fortnight. Heigh-ho. Shall we play?'

'Mm.'

Philip reluctantly readied himself to serve. Half an hour ago a gentle knockabout with his attractive landlady had seemed like a good idea, a welcome distraction from the nagging worries that beset him. But the tennis was shaping up as a massacre and the distractions showed no sign of receding. Since the weekend his mind had shifted perceptibly into a state of siege mentality.

'Love-fifteen.'

The play on its own was troubling enough. The production was adequate, his fellow actors excellent, his own performance as good as any he'd given in years, but doubts about his suitability for the role, as expressed by himself as much as by Dick Jones, had never gone away.

'Love-thirty.'

Dick Jones. A name to make a man's grip on his racket tighten in a parody of strangulation at the best of times. To be in a state of direct competition with the vile wretch was not to be borne; oh that it should ever come to keeping up with the Jones!

'Good shot, Philip! You certainly gave that one a whack! Fifteen-thirty.'

Word was that his performance in the studio theatre was first-rate. Of course it wasn't, it couldn't be, it was just a case of backstage buzz and hype, but now that the compassionate vote was mobilized in his favour there was no way he could lose. *Right or Wrong* was due to open the following Tuesday. Jones was making pathetic fake-deathbed noises about not knowing whether or not he'd be fit enough to perform, but he'd be out there whatever happened, glued to a sympathy wheelchair if need be. Who then would dare raise their pen against him?

'Fifteen-forty.'

And then no doubt he'd be smirking on the front cover of every newspaper the morning after, the game hero risen from death's door to carry the torch of his art. No doubt he'd be pictured leaning for support on the shoulder of his achingly pretty twentysomething girlfriend. Someone had tried to tell him the other day that he was completely mistaken about Dick and Sally, that they weren't an item at all, but that was obvious hogwash. He'd known they were together all along for a fact, his own source of information was impeccable. The press coverage merely confirmed what was public knowledge already. For all that, it had still made him feel ill.

'Phew! That was venomous, Philip. Thirty-forty.'

There was Jones with the gorgeous Sally on his arm, and here was Philip with – who? Olive? What a conquest! What a claim to fame. Apparently the wretched press photographer who'd turned up for the team photo had taken a long-range snap of Olive handing him her cake. It would be appearing in the local rag this week, no doubt with some suitable Godiva-like touching up, a humiliating addenda to the pages of promised rubbish on Dick and Sally. Dick and Sally. Sally and Dick. Sod the bloody lot of them.

'Deuce. Philip, what's got into you? That was a perfect ace!'

They were all under his skin, like grubs writhing. Oh goody, everyone had said after the run this morning, an afternoon off, yippee! No doubt they'd all be out denuding every florist in Chichester, queueing up behind Sally in time for hospital visiting, hoping the press corps might snatch enough of a concerned profile to permit a shallow bathe in the reflected glory. Bully for the bloody lot of them.

'Your advantage, Mr Fletcher. I say!'

There'd been no relaxing afternoon off for him. He'd endured the sweaty London train, both ways, a pointless journey designed only to confirm what he didn't want to know anyway. He'd been home to his study and unloaded the two cases of fan mail he kept under the spare bed. All human nuttiness was there, an exhaustive archive of the full unhinged spectrum of obsession. Not all the letters came under this umbrella, of course. Some were polite expressions of thanks for his performances, others contained intelligent commentaries on plays and programmes in which he had appeared, but there was also a solid vein

114

of pure barking lunacy, including no fewer than twenty-four proposals of marriage from complete strangers. Two of them came from Olive Vibash.

'Deuce.'

She'd been writing to him for years, he simply hadn't twigged. There were seven letters in all, and for all he knew there'd been more – he only kept about half those he received. They were strange epistles, full of passion and banality in equal measure, with more sexual innuendo than a *Carry On* film, and more recipes than an issue of *Woman's Own*. Olive was particularly into jam, and she was uninhibited about sharing her interest. During the course of her letters Philip learnt everything he'd never wanted to know about boiling fruit, adding sugar, bottling, storing, pastry making, jam sponges and blackberry tarts. It was mind-numbing stuff.

'Bad luck – my advantage.'

So why hadn't he remembered her before? The answer was both simple and horribly depressing. Olive had rung no bells because her outpourings were quite unexceptional. He had in his possession hundreds of letters no more or less nutty than hers, he had dozens of regular correspondents with obsessions distinguishable from hers and from each others' only in content and not in tone. The world was full of Olive and her ilk. The only wonder was that thus far she was the only one to have streaked directly across his life.

'Game. My serve. Four games to love.'

It was an image already burned indelibly into his mind. He hadn't slept well last night, and when at last he did drop off in the small hours he had dreamt of coming home and finding Olive waiting naked in his bed. Of what might he dream tonight? Of platoons, of whole companies of Olives parading for his attention? Of Olives not in single spies but in battalions?

He seemed to have lost another game. At any rate they

were changing ends again. He had to serve to save the set. Fat bloody chance of that. He lost.

'It's your injury, I expect,' said Jennifer sympathetically. 'They can be nasty, I know. In fact I've still got a bit of a shoulder strain myself.'

'I shouldn't like to play you when you've recovered.'

'I don't suppose you fancy another set?'

'No.'

'Then let's have a drink.'

It was an irresistible proposition. The sun was comfortably over the yardarm and Philip's thirst could not be quenched by mineral water alone. He was directed to the summer house while she went inside to mix some vodka martinis.

The summer house stood at the bottom of the garden, some distance from and almost out of sight of the house and tennis court. The glass windows had been absorbing heat all day and it was too hot to sit inside, though the sun was now low and the evening mild. In any case, the interior was cluttered, stacked with garden furniture, toys and a racing bicycle. Philip sat down instead on one of two sun loungers on the lawn outside. He was sitting with his elbows on his knees, staring at his spired fingers and thinking miserably of the play and Dick and Sally and Olive when Jennifer reappeared with a loaded tray.

She had changed out of her tennis costume. She was wearing a short white towelling robe, loosely, very loosely belted at the waist. As soon as she had given him his drink she took it off.

'I hope you don't mind,' she said, stretching herself out on the other lounger. She was wearing a yellow bikini that cannot have much depleted the manufacturer's stock of material. 'I'm a bit of a sun worshipper.'

It was an unfortunate time to be offering up her devotions. Such little sunlight as still prevailed penetrated only weakly the screen of trees to the west of the summer house. Philip's smile was suitably wan.

'I don't mind at all,' he said, taking a long cool sip of his drink. It was strong, it ought to have been invigorating. But he felt listless.

Jennifer reached down to the tray, which had contained not merely their drinks but also a tray of ice cubes, sunglasses and a little floral bag. From the bag she took out a tube of Ambre Solaire, which she began applying to her arms. It seemed an unnecessary precaution.

Philip watched her. His eyes wandered unchecked over the smooth tanned belly and thighs, rolled over the curve of her hips, the perfect swelling of her breasts. Her palms, refilled with oil, traced firm voluptuous circles on her stomach. He wondered if he'd ever witnessed such a blatant come-on in his life. He knew exactly what was coming next.

'You couldn't be an angel and do my back, could you?'

Angelic thoughts were far from both their minds. He came and perched on the edge of her lounger and rubbed oil into her lower back. She emitted a low breathy sound, somewhere between a sigh and a purr.

'Mm. Do the rest, please.'

Her eyes were closed, her lips slightly parted in a dreamy smile. She reached behind to undo her bra strap.

'Allow me.'

Philip unfastened with one hand while oiling between her shoulder blades with the other.

'Why, Mr Fletcher, you've done this before!'

'Once or twice.'

'Could you rub it harder – there.'

'Here?'

'Mm. That's good. My shoulder's so stiff.'

Somehow and inevitably the application of lotion had become a sensual massage. No final barrier of intimacy had yet been breached, no tacit acknowledgement of ulterior intention made, but a physical overture had begun with an implicit promise of crescendo. For now his hands remained in the vicinity of her shoulders, but it was understood that they were under licence to stray. Philip knew the rules, he'd played this game rather more than once or twice before. Besides, he couldn't help but notice that the little floral bag on the drinks tray contained an assortment of condoms.

'Mm, that's wonderful. It's so nice to be pampered. And it's so rare, these days. Children always demanding attention. If not them my husband.'

'Your kids are away too, eh?'

'Just for the night. Staying with their aunt. Lovely to have a bit of time to myself. Time to play. While the cat's away.'

He didn't suppose that she was thinking of tennis. His slippery fingers gently kneaded her shoulders. Though she lay quite still she was anything but inert, responding to his touch with obvious pleasure, conveying her arousal and availability with negative effort. She seemed utterly sure of herself, as she had every right to be, an attractive and sexually charged woman offering up her near-naked body in the certain conviction that no red-blooded male would refuse. How often, he wondered, did she do this? Were the husband's absences carefully ringed in a calendar, children accordingly despatched, her diversions as carefully calculated as today's? How many other men had been on this very lounger, ad hoc masseurs savouring the moment of delicious anticipation when they realized their luck was in? Perhaps it was a regular occurrence with her lodgers. Perhaps one day he would come across another actor who had stayed there, who would give him the nudge, the wink, and say 'Landlady obliges, old chum. LLO.' Every customer guaranteed satisfaction too, he didn't doubt. Why then did he feel so uninterested?

It wasn't as if he was sexually sated. Quite the opposite

118

– his sex life was nonexistent. Nor was Jennifer an unattractive prospect – quite the opposite there, too. But there was something wrong. Was it her obviousness? No, he'd never been squeamish and he had no problem with man-eaters. In any case, he was flattered that she still fancied him after his inept, unathletic display on the tennis court. But still there was a missing ingredient. The physiological signs were incontrovertible – he was showing no sign whatsoever of rising to the occasion.

His problem was simple. It was Olive. He couldn't get her out of his mind. All the time he'd been at the theatre that morning he'd been glancing over his shoulder, convinced that she'd be there. He'd been paranoid about her following him home. She was plaguing him; he could have joyfully throttled her. How in God's name could he think about sex, with Olive on the brain? It was a bromide for all seasons.

'I'm terribly sorry,' he said, snatching away his hands and rising suddenly from the lounger, 'but could I borrow your bicycle?'

'Could you what?'

She swivelled her upper body round to face him, a stunned look on her face in perfect accompaniment to the tone of her voice. He stared for a lingering, regretful moment at her newly uncovered breasts.

'The bicycle. In the summer house. Mind if I borrow it? Just for a few hours. I'll look after it. Promise.'

She didn't speak. She was clearly having trouble getting her head round what he'd just said. To save time, Philip decided to take her silence for assent.

'Good! That's very kind of you, I'm most grateful.'

He darted into the summer house, moved some chairs to clear a path and wheeled out the racing bicycle. The chain looked as if it could do with some oil, but the tyres were firm and it appeared to be in good condition.

'That's brilliant,' he told her. 'Just what I needed. Thank

you so much for the tennis. Let's do it again. Soon.'

Still she didn't speak. She was in exactly the same position, her weight rested on one elbow, her face as blank and pale as an accident victim's. She hadn't moved when he glanced down at the lawn from his bedroom window a minute or so later.

He was in his bedroom for a little over ten minutes, ample time in which to skim through his make-up box and effect a minor disguise. A trim dark goatee beard and matching sideburns set the tone. He ruddied his cheeks a little, to suggest weathering, and selected some metal-rimmed spectacles from his plain-lensed collection. He put on a pullover over his tennis shirt, but didn't change his white shorts and shoes. He completed the ensemble with a floppy white hat which he had bought on Saturday for the cricket but not worn. It was not a disguise to thwart close scrutiny, but from a distance he had no doubt that he could pass for a bird-watcher or a country rambler. He had a pair of binoculars to supply the finishing touch.

Jennifer had gone in by the time he was finished, so he sneaked down from his flat surreptitiously, picked up the bicycle from the foot of the staircase, and cut round the side of the house to avoid the drive. He threaded his way through the trees to the front gate. Once outside he mounted the bicycle and headed off in the direction of Goodwood.

He hadn't been on a bicycle for years, but a minute sufficed to prove the adage that it was a skill once mastered and never lost. The country was to all intents and purposes flat and the journey in the cool of the evening thankfully effortless. He rode first to Lavant, then turned off in the direction of Goodwood at the first sign. He took as his landmark the Trundle, an Iron-Age hill fort near to the racetrack that dominated the surrounding landscape. He didn't know where he was going, and supposed that after a while he would just have to stop and ask, but a mile or so from Lavant he struck lucky. At a fork in the road, where he paused for a moment unsure whether to head left or right, he saw a small faded sign attached to a post. It read HERON FARM – 200 YARDS.

He followed the road for a hundred yards, then turned . off at the entrance to a bright yellow rape field. He left the bicycle just inside the gate, and skirted round the edge of the field. He could see the roof of a building poking out from a little hollow and, beyond, smoke rising above some trees.

He would have been hard put to explain exactly what he was doing. He supposed, in psychospeak terms, he was confronting his own fear. Not that he was actually planning to beard Olive directly – hence the disguise – but perhaps by invading her territory, by staking her out and fixing her in her own context he might find some focus for his unease. He needed to locate her in some metaphorical sense. It might prove to have practical benefits too. Though he had no scheme for dealing with her in the long term, should he conceive of one a general recce would be invaluable.

He approached the first building cautiously. It was a small cottage, charming and rustic from a distance but marred close up by an ugly modern extension at the rear. It seemed deserted. It was coming up to nine o'clock, and though it was still light the dusk was thickening by the minute. The cottage interior was dark. He walked around it, peering through the small leaded windows. He could only see into the extension, which had bigger windows and an all-glass door at the back. He saw a kitchen. There were cereal packets out on the table and a pile of unwashed crockery in the sink. He didn't think Goldilocks would have been tempted.

He followed a narrow muddy track that began at the front door of the cottage and ran along a rough S-bend through some trees. At the second bend the ground sloped sharply upwards. He saw lights ahead.

The path came out at a stretch of open land so rutted and churned by countless vehicles that it was almost a morass. A pair of tractors and a battered Range Rover stood parked in a line on the other side as if surveying their handiwork. Beyond them was a clump of outbuildings and a substantial walled farmhouse. The smoke he had seen earlier was coming from its chimney. Lights were on downstairs.

He skirted the clearing and passed behind a barn that shielded him from the house. He climbed the wall at a conveniently low point and found himself in an apple orchard. He picked his way through the trees, quietly opened a gate and came to some greenhouses. Beyond was a kitchen garden which extended all the way to the back of the house, a distance of about thirty yards. No lights were on at this side.

He crossed the kitchen garden rapidly. Although this end of the house was dark he stooped to avoid the windows as he felt his way along the wall. He peeked round the corner and saw a deserted farmyard. He hesitated. It occurred to him that if there was a farmyard there must at least be the possibility of a dog. He didn't much care for dogs and was distinctly unnerved at the thought of one snapping viciously at his heels. He checked for possible escape routes. If he couldn't get back the way he'd come he would just have to make a dash for the five-barred gate that led out to the boggy clearing. Unless it was a very slow dog he didn't think he'd have much of a chance.

Thoughts of canine mutilation notwithstanding, he crept across the front of the house. Beyond the front door was a lighted window. The curtain was drawn, he couldn't see inside. He moved on to the next window, which was open. As he approached he heard voices.

He was puzzled. The voices seemed familiar, one in particular. He approached the window on tiptoe, straining to listen. As he drew level he noticed the flicker of a TV screen, and in that moment he understood exactly why he recognized that voice – it was his own.

Olive was sitting with her back to the window watching a video. On screen, Philip, in the grey beard of old Sir Walter Raleigh, was shedding tears over the body of his son, young Walter, an actor whom Philip chiefly remembered for his uncontrolled flatulence. The scene was allegedly taking place on the deck of a ship, even more allegedly off the coast of Central America. The reality, a studio in Television Centre, had been scarcely disguised by the overstretched budget.

He'd made a pretty good job of it though, he couldn't help but reflect. His Walter Raleigh had been his big break, it was a performance of which he would always be unashamedly proud. He paused for a moment to appreciate it once more.This was one of a number of scenes he'd got faultlessly in one take, in this case weeping copiously on cue without benefit of onion and simulating grief so convincingly as to leave scarcely a dry eye among the hard-bitten crew. Or so, at any rate, he had always fondly believed. He stood contentedly at the window, no more than three feet from the back of Olive's head, while they both admired him.

Olive blew her nose loudly. She turned her head to the side for a moment as she looked for another tissue, and Philip saw that her cheeks were wet with tears. She cleared her nostrils with a second, mighty blow, and turned her attention back to the television.

Philip was stunned. In the moment of registering Olive's distress he had been seized involuntarily by an overwhelming and quite alien sensation of compassion. He felt decidedly shaken. A fervent antisentimentalist to his icy core, he couldn't remember the last time he'd felt such gross Dickensian sympathy for a fellow human being. Even worse, he experienced a spasm of something akin to guilt. Not half an hour before he had been thinking malevolently that he could throttle this woman; now his heart almost bled for her.

The fact that he even had a heart was a closely guarded secret. He felt like the smug chatelaine of an impregnable fortress staring into a breach. This woman loved him. To call her plain and overweight would be polite, to suggest she was perhaps a little crazy conservative, but she loved him. How many times had she watched this video? He could see a whole stack of them on a shelf behind the TV; he didn't doubt for a moment that he featured in them all. What had he ever done to deserve such unflinching devotion? He felt unworthy.

Unworthy and, for the first time in countless years, humble. He was awash with unexpected emotions tonight. There was a lump in his throat. He hadn't felt this bad since bawling his schoolboy eyes out at the death of Bambi's mother.

He and Olive watched the episode to the end. It was nearly dark by the time the video tape ran out. It was the final part, ending with Walter Raleigh's trial and execution. Olive went through a whole box of tissues; she was sobbing so loudly Philip could hardly hear himself speak. At one point he only just stopped himself from asking her to keep her voice down.

Just as the final credits rolled he heard the sound of a car. It seemed to be drawing nearer. Olive must have heard it too, for she first pricked up her ears, then twisted her head suddenly towards the window. Philip darted back out of sight. It was time he was off.

He retraced his steps round to the back of the house, through the kitchen garden and the orchard. There was barely enough light for him to see his way. The car had definitely been heading in this direction; as he approached the orchard gate he heard a door slam. He waited for a minute before climbing over the wall.

A white van was parked next to the Range Rover and tractors. No one was around, so he presumed that the driver had gone into the farmhouse. He didn't fancy going back the way he'd come, it was too dark on the windy path beneath the trees, so he crossed to the other side of the clearing and picked out the track that ran directly to the main road. He turned left and after some stumbling around the hedges succeeded in locating his bicycle. He set off for home.

He didn't have lights, it was a hairy ride, but he made it back in one piece despite twice riding into a ditch. He removed his unnecessary disguise at the top of the drive, and wheeled the bicycle back up to the house as quietly as he could, hoping not to be noticed. Unfortunately he tripped the security light as he came into the courtyard and Jennifer saw him. She was standing in the kitchen talking on the telephone. He waved at her shyly. She gave a perfunctory wave back and walked away out of sight, still speaking into the phone.

He experienced a momentary twinge, as anyone might who finds himself staring at a retreating gift horse. Then he affected a shrug. There would be other Jennifers. Tonight he had hunted an altogether rarer quarry. It had been a strange pursuit, it had surprised and shocked him, but in a curious way he wasn't able to define it had left him feeling satisfied. He still didn't know how he would deal with Olive when (and he was certain it was a question of when and not if) their paths crossed again, but he had quite overcome his disquiet and he felt confident that he would be able to face her with equanimity. He was embarrassed that he had always been so blasé about his fans. Just because he was a successful and talented actor there was no reason to forget those less fortunate than himself, those who, collectively, performed the role of appreciative chorus. What was an actor without his audience? Who was Philip without his fans? No wonder he had experienced the unaccustomed strains of humility.

He went to bed with a light heart. He was opening a new play in inauspicious circumstances, he might have expected to lie awake nervously, but he dropped off almost instantly. He slept like a baby, and no threatening dreams disturbed him.

10

On opening night Sally arrived at the theatre with even more than the usual trepidation. The preview had gone well enough, but the long week had been draining and she had had no time to herself in which to focus her concentration. The press continued to hound her. One paper, ludicrously, had carried the story that she was secretly engaged to Dick Jones, and by the next edition it was being repeated in all the gossip columns. Though she had heard of journalistic licence she was nonetheless astonished to discover how shamelessly it aped the precepts of fiction. She had asked her agent to issue a statement denying any romantic involvement with Dick or with anyone else, but it had been ignored. Their attitude seemed to be that she would say that, wouldn't she? – and in the meantime they were selling papers. Everyone involved was feeling the pressure, not least the police, who were under fire for not having caught the van driver. She had wasted a precious hour that afternoon down at the station looking at mugshots of local villains. It had proved, as expected, a pointless exercise (as far as she was concerned it could have been any or none of them) but she supposed that they had to be seen to be doing something. They even wanted her to appear on *Crimewatch*, which was ironic. She had once auditioned unsuccessfully for the role of a rape victim in one of their dramatic reconstructions.

127

She got to the theatre two hours before the half and parked on the fenced-in strip of land by the football pitch. By arriving so early she hoped to get in unnoticed, but as she approached the stage door she saw that a crowd had already gathered. Philip Fletcher was amongst them, holding forth expansively and signing autographs. She was surprised, as he was notoriously businesslike with fans. She was grateful, though, for the distraction. She slipped away unseen and retraced her steps round to the rear of the theatre. There was a white gate that led into the garden terrace outside the Green Room, and, thankfully, it was open. She made her way to her dressing room.

It looked like a florist's overflow zone. Bouquets and pots and baskets smothered every surface, and when her dresser popped her head in to say hello she learnt that there were more at the stage door. Dozens of cards were piled on her table, and in the course of the next few hours many more arrived. Her visitors were kind but distracting. She had her own obligatory contribution to make to the first night game, and wasted a long quarter of an hour doing the rounds and handing out good luck messages. The atmosphere backstage was thick with nervous tension and excitement. She went out front to try and escape it, but the crew were still working on the set and there was no peace and quiet to be found on stage. In vain she sought refuge in her dressing room. The trickle of visitors continued unabated. Philip Fletcher was one of the last. He arrived just before the half-hour already made up and dressed, in a gold-brocaded waistcoat, breeches and white silk stockings, and a knee-length scarlet coat. Sally complimented him on his appearance.

'Why thank you. And thanks too for your card. Please accept a small token of good luck.'

He produced a ribbon-wrapped bottle of champagne. She cleared a space for it on her table.

'Philip, that's incredibly kind.'

'Don't mention it, my dear.' He glanced with a wry smile at the floral display. 'I'm glad I didn't choòse flowers.' He sniffed at a white rose in a bursting arrangement, prominently displayed. 'From Dick? How is he, by the way?'

It was a good thing she had a rosy rustic make-up; she felt the flush at her cheeks. Dick had sent her flowers, but not those ones, which had arrived without a card.

'I don't know who they're from,' she answered, though she had her suspicions. 'Dick's fine, I think – I haven't seen him since Monday.'

She'd ruled out further hospital visits after being bushwacked by reporters on the way out. It had not been a pleasant experience. She knew no more about the state of Dick's health than any of them, which was basically that he was okay but was staying in for a few days either as a sensible precaution or as a bid for sympathy and attention, depending on which way one looked at it. Either way, she was irritated to the quick at being universally misconstrued at Dick's *amour*. The only *amour* in Dick's life was of the *propre* variety.

'Look, Philip, I don't know how this rumour's – '

'Fifteen minutes, ladies and gentlemen,' announced the tannoy. 'This is your quarter-hour call.'

'Can I come in?' said Martha, her dresser, squeezing past Philip.

'You wanted to see the dress-rehearsal photos,' said the production manager, also appearing at the door. He put down a thick red folder on the cluttered table and retreated back to the corridor. 'I'll collect them at the interval.'

'Wouldn't mind a look at them myself later,' said Philip pleasantly, turning to go. 'I'd better go and get my wig on. See you out there!'

He closed the door after him. Sally slipped into her first costume, a pretty but simple dress suitable for a country wife.

129

'He's in a chirpy mood then,' murmured Martha suspiciously.

'Philip?'

'Mm.' She set to buttoning Sally's dress. 'You should have heard him ten minutes ago. Proper little prima donna.'

'Complaining?'

'Mm. Not happy with his cossie one bit. I'm glad I'm not dressing him.'

'His costume looks fine.'

'It's his corset.'

'He's wearing a corset? What on earth for?'

'Vanity, dear. If you ask me it's a miracle he can even breathe. You should have seen him before he put his shirt on. Looked more trussed up than a Christmas turkey.'

Sally's telephone rang. She answered it reluctantly.

'Hello?'

There was silence at the other end. She spoke again, but there was no reply. She waited for a count of five before putting the receiver down.

'No one there?' said Martha.

'No.'

'Could be a cock-up at the switchboard; they've been having problems all week. Need a hand with the shoes?'

She did. Nothing about her clothes was simple, there were hooks, eyes and buttons everywhere. Her changes would be tedious, but she wasn't complaining. All of the costumes were wonderful. So was the set. All that was in question was the acting. And the test of that was fast approaching.

'Ladies and gentlemen, this is your Act I beginners call . . .'

Martha had gone, she listened on her own to the tannoy. She heard the loud excited buzz of the audience dropping to sudden silence as the lights blacked out, then the opening music, a specially arranged Corelli quartet.

130

After a moment Philip's voice came in strongly with the first line and the play was underway. The exposition was brisk and clear, Philip sounded on top form, the audience was hushed and attentive. Then Roy entered, crabbed and abrasive (a naturalistic actor to his fingertips), and the laughs started to come. They were going at a hell of a lick, the scenes seemed to fly by. Before she knew it she was hearing Robert's voice, then she knew with a shock she'd be on soon. She anticipated her call and went down early for the beginning of Act II.

An ASM was there, connected by headphones with the DSM out front. Sally stood woodenly waiting for her cue, going over her opening lines, which for seconds that seemed like hours she couldn't remember. Maggie Carter came and joined her. They squeezed hands and pretended not to be nervous. They heard the applause for the end of the first act and saw their cue light go green. They went through the door, and up the steps of the right-hand vomatorium as the lights came up. They saw the top of Julian's head, then heard the titter of laughter that told them he had performed his camp little mime and hidden himself behind a screen. Now Sally could feel the audience, she could even see some of them out of the corners of her eyes, but she kept her attention fixed firmly ahead, tripped gaily up the three last steps to the stage and turned back with full wide-eyed exuberance to say:

'Pray, sister, where are the best fields and woods to walk in, in London?'

Maggie had stopped to address an aside to the audience while Sally continued across the vast open stage. Inside she had been quivering, but she'd heard her voice ring out loud and clear. The adrenaline flowed and almost instantly her nerves decamped. She threw herself into the scene con brio.

Julian came forward, his thin face a constipated mask of suspicion and jealousy. The audience clearly loved him, and he lapped up their approval. The theatre was buzzing, everyone was full of zest. At the end of the scene there was a burst of applause. Chichester first nights were like that.

Sally's second scene went just as well. When she came off she headed straight for one of the ground-floor dressing rooms, which had been designated a quick change area. Martha was waiting with her change of costume, the blue velvet suit that was her Act III masculine disguise. While Martha did her buttons she recombed her hair and adjusted her broad-brimmed plumed hat. She raced back to the vomatorium buckling on her sword belt.

As soon as she came on she realized that they had the audience in the palms of their hands. The other actors knew it too, their mutual confidence was unbounded as they surfed the waves of laughter. At the end of the act, which was the interval, they came off hugging each other with delight.

When Sally got back to her dressing room, Martha was waiting for her with a cup of tea.

'Antonia was asking for you.'

'I'll pop in in a sec. Give me a hand, will you?'

Together they got her out of her costume. A stream of visitors arrived in quick succession, all highly excited. The last was the company manager.

'Had a look at the photos yet?'

She hadn't. She looked on the table for the red folder. It wasn't there.

'I'm sorry,' she said. 'Looks like someone's taken them.'

'Probably Philip,' he answered. 'Never mind. I'll go and ask him.'

Just as Martha finished buttoning her dress the telephone rang. Sally answered it while combing her hair. She got no reply.

'Dead again?' asked Martha. 'I bet it's something funny

with the switchboard. I'll have a word with them when I go down.'

'Don't bother,' said Sally. 'I'll go myself.'

'No, I'll go. You finish your tea.'

She'd barely finished drinking it when the tannoy call came for second-half beginners. She remembered that Antonia had been asking for her. Their two dressing rooms had interconnecting doors, so she knocked and went on in. Antonia was sitting stiffly in her chair reading a magazine, a matronly vision in black and imperial purple.

'*Très formidable*,' said Sally cheerfully. 'I can quite see you as Lady Bracknell.'

'I shall refuse to play it unless you're cast as Gwendoline, my dear,' said the old lady gracefully. 'It's going rather well, isn't it? Or shouldn't I say that?'

'Probably not. Martha said you wanted to see me.'

Antonia looked blank.

'Do I?'

Sally laughed.

'She said you were asking for me. Before the interval.'

For another moment Antonia continued to look blank, then recollection glimmered in her eyes.

'Oh yes. Did you see your friend?'

'My friend?'

'Yes, he was asking after you. He was in your dressing room. I heard him, you see, I thought it was you. I went in to say good luck, but it wasn't you at all. He didn't give his name, I'm sorry.'

'I'm sorry, too,' said Sally laughing, 'but I'm afraid you've lost me. There was somebody asking after me, but you don't know who it was?'

'I know, I'm a silly old thing, please forgive me, my dear, but I was a bit surprised to find this chap in your dressing room. It's none of my business, I know, but I wanted to check that it was all right. He said he was waiting for you.'

133

'You're quite right to check; thank you. What did he look like?'

'Oh, difficult to say. Quite ordinary. That's not very helpful, is it?'

'Was he fair, quite thin, about six feet?'

'Oh no. Quite dark. Not that tall. Perhaps a bit on the stocky side. Oh, and he was wearing black clothes.'

Sally let out a small sigh of relief. Although the description remained pretty vague, it clearly hadn't been who she thought it might be.

'I expect it was one of the stage crew, Antonia.'

'Oh, of course. They all wear black, don't they? How silly of me.'

'Not at all. He probably wanted to give me some technical note. I really should lock my dressing room, though. You never know who's about, do you? See you out there. I've got to dash.'

She had plenty of time, but she wanted to listen from the beginning of the act, to check that neither the actors nor audience had gone off the boil. They hadn't. At the end of the scene there was another swell of applause. Julian took her hand and they made their way on stage in the blackout. The next scene, a long two-hander between the two of them, went better than it had ever done. When she came off she ran to her dressing room to change her costume and then rushed back to watch her favourite bit of the play.

It was the famous scene where Sir Jasper catches his wife in the arms of Horner, but is persuaded that as he's a eunuch his intentions are innocent and that she is merely collecting from him a piece of 'china'. The double entendres fly thick and fast, but the sheer verve and brazen implausibility of the writing make it one of the funniest scenes in English drama. The principal players, even the unbearable Roy, had been delightful during

134

rehearsal. With an audience as responsive as this one it was a scene that ought to bring the house down.

It did. Sally arrived in time to see Antonia's dread-nought-like entrance and her exchange with Roy and Marianne. Philip and Dawn came tumbling out through one of the upstage doors, looking suitably dishevelled.

'And I have been toiling and moiling for the prettiest piece of china, my dear,' gasped Dawn, offering for general inspection a delicate blue saucer. They occupied the long ensuing pause for laughter in discreetly readjusting their clothes. Roy, with rather less discretion, mimed taking in snuff. Marianne crossed the stage to try and interpose herself between Philip and Dawn.

'. . . Good Mr Horner, don't think to give other people china and me none; come in with me too.'

'Upon my honour, I have none left now.'

Philip affected innocence while the two women squabbled over him. Eventually Marianne grabbed at his coat to drag him offstage. According to the stage directions she 'pulls him by the cravat', but in rehearsal Philip had worried about being throttled so they had changed it to his lapel. Unfortunately she missed, and somehow pulled off his wig.

It was a hideous moment. The wig was an elaborate arrangement of thick shoulder-length dark curls that made Philip look like the Laughing Cavalier. But when it came off, revealing the ungainly stocking cap that was keeping his own hair in place, he looked rather more like the Miserable Roundhead. He made a desperate instinctive grab for the wig which Marianne, instantly overcome with shock and horror, had dropped like a hot coal. Philip missed, stumbled over her leg, and fell to the floor.

The laughter had ceased, to be replaced by nervous tit-ters and embarrassed silence. The actors exchanged frozen glances, not quite sure what to do. Dawn, quicker-witted than the rest, hurried across to retrieve the wig and handed it back to Philip, who, still kneeling, hastily shoved it back on his head. It wasn't straight, there were more titters. The pause, which had thus far been about ten seconds, seemed to have lasted for as many minutes. The actors stared anxiously at each other, desperate for the next line.

It was Antonia's. Like the others she had frozen over, but when she realized that they were all looking at her, and depending on her to retrieve the scene, she appeared to cease breathing altogether. She stared numbly down at Philip. He gazed back imploringly. Something clicked inside her brain.

'Mr Worthing! Rise, sir, from this semi-recumbent posture. It is most indecorous.'

There was an almost audible clunking noise as everyone's jaw hit the floor at the same time. The collective intake of breath from the audience seemed to leave a vacuum on stage. If a hole had appeared miraculously in the ground the actors would have fought amongst themselves for the right to jump into it first.

'O lord, here's a man!' declared Dawn suddenly, unilaterally cutting some ten lines and racing down to where Julian was due to make his next appearance. Julian hastened on to the stage. Roy was slow at picking up his cue, but nonetheless they succeeded somehow in getting the play back on track. Almost immediately, Dawn exited, followed by Roy, Antonia and Marianne. They staggered down to the vom where Sally was watching, looking like they'd seen a ghost.

'I'm sorry,' gasped Antonia. 'I'm so, so sorry.'

'Never mind, dear,' said Dawn, mechanically soothing. 'I'm sure nobody noticed.'

Roy snorted furiously. Dawn hissed at him. As soon as they were through the door and out of earshot the two of them launched into a vicious argument.

'Let's go back to your dressing room,' said Sally hastily,

taking Antonia's arm and leading her away from the scene of carnage. 'I'll get you a nice cup of tea.'

In the event it was Martha who did the tea while Sally rushed back to be in time for her next entrance. The scene went smoothly enough, but the atmosphere in the theatre had been fatally contaminated. When she came off she found that it had spread backstage, where there was a general air of shell shock. The wonderful effervescent confidence that had lifted the evening on to a magical plane had vanished. Everyone knew it, and no one knew what to do about it.

They rallied and managed to infuse the last act with a spirit of grim determination. It was not, alas, the quality most needed for a comedy. They got through it efficiently enough, there were even some good laughs, but the savour had gone and the aftertaste was flat. The audience, liberally speckled with friends and supporters, did their best at the curtain call, but the valiant cheering was as hollow as the actors' smiles. They knew that a single catastrophic moment had derailed a brilliant success.

Afterwards Antonia and Marianne were inconsolable; each was convinced that the disaster had been solely her fault. So too, in his own way, was Philip. His wig had been so well moulded, and had felt so secure, that he hadn't bothered to glue it down. Passers-by in the corridor outside his dressing room heard him raving and pitied whoever it was who was on the receiving end of his ire, but it turned out that he was on his own and shouting at himself. Dawn remarked that he had always been notorious for talking to himself, even in his student days.

Dawn was doing valiant work among the walking wounded, despite having her husband to look after. The husband, a quiet and immensely successful businessman who manifestly felt like a fish out of water backstage, was left to stew while Dawn gathered up Antonia and Marianne and cajoled them mercilessly into cheering up.

Both had declared their intention to skip the first-night party, but Dawn wouldn't hear of it. She came to knock on Sally's door before escorting her swollen party over the road to the theatre restaurant.

'Coming?'

'In a minute. I'll see you there.'

Sally sat at her dressing table and listened as the corridor outside emptied. She had been dreading this moment for weeks; the second-half disaster merely added to her foreboding. The production was up and running now, rehearsals were over and after a handful of performances the play would be going into repertory. That meant nights off, free time which everyone else had been anticipating eagerly but which she had been dreading. Starting tonight, she would have to get on with her life.

She didn't want to go to the party. She didn't want to be on her own either, but enforced bonhomie was less appealing than solitude. She had decided to wait until everyone else had gone over, and then to slip away unnoticed.

The telephone rang. The sudden noise startled her, it made her heart beat faster. She hesitated before picking up the receiver.

'Hello?' she said reluctantly.

There was silence at the other end. She sat very still, hardly daring to breathe. Her palms were sweating and her mouth was dry. There had been two ring-offs earlier in the evening. She had tried so hard to believe Martha's explanation of a faulty switchboard. It couldn't be starting again, could it?

'Hello?' she repeated faintly. 'Anyone there?'

A tiny click sounded in her ear.

'Sal, is that you?'

The voice was thin and distant. It took her a moment to recognize it.

'Lizzie!'

138

The tension flooded out of her. She gave a near-hysterical laugh.

'You all right, Sal?'

'Fine. It's lovely to hear from you.'

'Thank God I got hold of you at last. I was trying earlier, kept getting cut off. Bloody phone boxes. I wanted to wish you all the best. Bit bloody late now.'

'No, it's very sweet of you. Thanks for your card.'

'How did it go?'

'Oh, *comme ci comme ça*. Bit of a cock-up in the fourth act, but apart from that it was okay. How's yours going?'

'Let's change the subject. I've got another reason for ringing, I'm afraid. Jason's been trying to get hold of you.'

'Oh God . . . Did you speak to him?'

'No, he left a message on the answerphone. It's not very pleasant, I'm afraid. I know this is not the sort of thing you want to hear when you're trying to unwind and have a good time, but as I say, I thought you ought to know.'

'Is the message still on?'

'Yes. That's the pips, I don't have any more coins. I'll try and call again tomorrow.'

'Thanks, Liz.'

She put down the phone and sank back listlessly into her chair. She had known this was going to happen; known it and tried to ignore it, along with all that other flotsam and jetsam collecting in the mire of her subconscious. She saw her white, drained face in the mirror and couldn't suppress an ironic smile. It wasn't turning out to be a great night.

Jason had been a mistake. Her private life had been filled with mistakes, but Jason had been an error on a capital scale: moody, paranoid, jealously obsessive, neurotically unbalanced and a crap actor to boot. He hadn't been able to handle her success, their six months together had been one long protracted sulk. She couldn't believe that they'd lasted that long. Yet somehow he'd made her feel guilty at ending their relationship. He had implied that she wanted out only because he was a failure, that she wanted no bit-part player on her arm to sully her starry glow, that, in short, she was a selfish monster who would let no common human sentiment come between her and her outsize ego. She hadn't denied it. What was the point? He was beyond reason, consumed by wild illogical passions. One moment he was sobbing at her feet, the next he had his hands round her throat and was threatening to kill her. Lizzie had seen the marks, she had wanted to call the police, but Sally had refused to let her. The next day a huge bouquet of yellow and white roses had arrived, with a pitiful note begging her to ring him. She had never rung, nor seen him since.

But he'd been lurking somewhere in the back of her mind all this time. She couldn't say she was surprised to hear from him. Perhaps it had been a case of a sixth sense, but when Antonia had told her about the man in her dressing room she had thought immediately of Jason. The anonymous bouquet of yellow and white roses had had his hallmark too, but she doubted that he would have made a peace-offering of her favourite flowers and an angry call on the same day. She wondered just what he had said. There was only one way to find out.

She picked up the phone again and dialled her own number. When the answerphone bleep came on, she tapped in the code and listened to the tape. Jason's was the only message.

It wasn't as bad as she had feared. The worst part was hearing his voice again after all this time. He was screaming at the start, calling her a slag, a bitch, a cow, spicing his abuse with every expletive under the sun. After half a minute or so he calmed down and became merely sarcastic. He wasn't very coherent, but she inferred that the police had been to interview him, that they'd given him a hard time, that it was all part of her scheme of revenge.

He ended on a self-pitying note, wanting to know what he had ever done that was so wrong but love her? He demanded that she ring him and left a Birmingham number. He said he had an acting job.

She looked at the piece of paper on which she had mechanically written down the Birmingham number. It was too late to ring now, but she didn't think she would have called whatever the hour. She couldn't face talking to him. It would be pointless trying to explain that the police were merely making routine enquiries, that she had told them categorically that he wasn't the man they were after. He was bound not to believe her, bound to think that she had deliberately and maliciously set them on to him to get her own back. She had never thought for a moment that it had been him. The simple fact of the matter was that Jason had too much pride. And if he had been capable of making the anonymous calls, which he wasn't, he could never in a million years have committed the burglary. He didn't have the guts.

Somebody else had done that, someone she was sure they would never find. She had heard nothing more from the police herself, she doubted that they were even pursuing the case. It had taken them a month to track down Jason, and that smacked of tokenism. Now that they had been seen to do their duty they would no doubt forget about the whole affair. Unfortunately she couldn't.

She turned off the lights and locked the door. With an unwholesome mix of images and Jason's angry tones vying for attention inside her head she knew that sleep would not come easily tonight. She thought she would go home and get drunk. She headed for the stage door.

The corridor was deserted. She supposed that everyone must have left by now, but as she approached Philip's dressing room she noticed that his door was still open. She glanced in and saw him sitting in front of the mirrors,

141

his feet crossed and up on the table. He was leaning back dangerously in his chair caressing a large Scotch.

'Hello there,' he drawled amiably. 'Why aren't you at the party?'

'I could say the same.'

'True enough. I'm not really a party person, though I was just thinking that I ought to go and stick my head in for five minutes. I'm afraid I don't feel like being jolly tonight.'

'Me neither.'

'Well then, why don't you come in and have a drink with me?'

As star dressing rooms went it was by no means huge, but it was big enough to contain a couch and a comfortable armchair. She took the chair while he poured her a whisky.

'That's fine, thanks, I'm driving.'

'The motor car is the curse of the drinking classes. It's probably for that reason I've never owned one.'

'It must save you a lot of money.'

'On the contrary, it costs me a fortune. Most of my salary here has gone on taxi fares. Not that there's much else to spend it on in Chichester. I'm here as part of a rest cure. It's merely coincidental that our audience gives off the same impression.'

'They were pretty good tonight.'

'So they were. Very loud applause at the end, they gave it their best shot. A pity.'

There was a half-inch of neat Scotch in his glass. He knocked it back and poured an instant refill. He lit a cigarette.

'I didn't think you smoked,' said Sally.

'I hadn't touched one till tonight for a couple of months, I've been very good. But I'm only ever an ex-smoker, I've given up deluding myself that I'm a non-smoker. The strain of sanctimoniousness is too exhausting.'

'You're sounding almost Wildean, Mr Fletcher.'

'As he remarked about smoking, "Giving up is easy, I've done it hundreds of times" . . . It's topical to quote Oscar tonight.'

'Poor Antonia. You know, I feel that it's all my fault. I told her at the interval she looked like Lady Bracknell. She must have had a brainstorm.'

'It happens. I had a friend years ago (he swears this is true) was on stage with Ralph Richardson in, I think, *The Alchemist* – it was a Jonson anyway – and suddenly out of nothing Ralph comes in with a chunk of Prospero: "Ye elves of hills, brooks and dales . . ." Everyone just stops dead and stares at him, he stares back, seemingly as amazed as any of them, but carries on right through the speech, no doubt on the old Mastermind principle of "I've started so I'll finish." Nothing anyone could do.'

'And what happened then?'

'They got on with the play. Astonishingly enough the audience didn't seem to notice. I think they noticed tonight, though. It wasn't Antonia's fault, it was mine. I should have had my wits about me. And I should have glued my bloody wig on.'

He gestured as if to stub out his cigarette against the wig block on the table. The offending mass of close-knit curls, beautifully arranged, was sitting up pertly like a minor Crufts champion.

'I know it sounds lame,' said Sally, 'but I'll say it anyway: these things are never as bad as they seem.'

'You're right, it does sound lame. I know one must keep a sense of proportion, but given a choice between tenancy of the stage here tonight and the steerage deck of the *Titanic* it would probably come down to a points decision.'

'That sounds a little over-dramatic, Philip.'

'I'm an actor, for Christ's sake. I'm allowed to be over-dramatic!'

She thought he was cross, but after a moment he

laughed, and he sounded as if he meant it. Still she wasn't entirely sure. He kept his cards so close to his chest that it was hard to tell where the actor stopped and the man began. Of course that was true of many in the profession, but it was a pool that was overcrowded at the shallow end, and in most cases what you saw was what you got. Philip had an enigmatic quality. Whether it was natural or cultivated was a moot point, but there was more to him than mere rampant egotism. She had thought that he and Dick were two sides of the same coin, but now she wasn't so sure. There was probably less to Dick than met the eye, while Philip, to hijack his own metaphor, probably had more in common with the iceberg than the *Titanic*.

'Of course tonight wasn't my first on-stage disaster,' he said with a wry chuckle. He pulled a face and put on a black-and-white comedy character voice: ''Oh no missus, not by a long chalk . . .'' I had the mother of all dries in Bristol twenty years ago. But I expect Dick's told you about that. It was only –'

'Why should Dick have told me about it?'

Her tone was brusque, he seemed surprised. He hadn't really been looking at her, he was still facing out of the door with his feet on the table, but he looked at her now. He had an eyebrow almost comically arched.

'I'm sorry?'

'I'm not having an affair with Dick Jones, Philip.'

The eyebrow remained in position. He sat fixed, watching and listening intently.

'Not only have I not been having an affair with Dick Jones, even the thought of having one would be unlikely to cross my mind in – what shall we say? – a thousand years. No, let's make that a million. I have a flat upstairs from him, I have had a lift in his car, and I was his dinner companion the night he was attacked. That is all. Period.'

Philip took a long drag of his cigarette while he thought

144

about it. His face was composed and expressionless, but his eyes were keen and alert. He nodded slowly to himself.

'You know, I once read in a gossip column that I was engaged to an actress I'd never even met. Funny how rumours take hold, isn't it?'

'No, it's not funny really. It's a pain in the neck. Thanks for the drink. I think I'll be going.'

'To the party?'

'I don't think so.'

She put down her glass. Philip at last took his feet off the table.

'See you tomorrow then. Oh, Sally . . .'

She was about to go through the door. She stopped.

'Did I overhear you saying that you didn't go back to town at weekends?'

'Yes.'

'Me neither. Would you care to have dinner after the show tomorrow?'

Well that didn't take long, she thought. She stalled.

'I'm not sure, I may have friends down. Can I let you know tomorrow?'

'Of course. If not Saturday, any time. Except Monday. My agent's coming on Monday, he bores for England and I wouldn't dream of inflicting him on you. Unless you get *much* better notices than me.'

She returned his smile. She was thinking that it was hard not to like him, which she realized was an odd thought to be having in view of his persistently irritating behaviour all during rehearsals. To be sure he had charm to spare, but that wasn't it. She found Philip Fletcher intriguing, she always had done. *Antony and Cleopatra* at the Riverside last year had been her first big theatre job. After a couple of years of rep and minor tours she'd suddenly found herself in the company of famous actors, and she'd been not a little in awe of them. Philip had seemed like a perfect model of an experienced classical actor:

145

confident and amusing, intelligent and perceptive, impressively focused and controlled; quite handsome too, in a conservative sort of way. She thought that she had probably had a kind of girlish crush on him. She was glad that she had cleared the air with him tonight and she had every intention of accepting his dinner invitation. At the very least she wanted to know how his technique would compare with Dick's. Somehow she didn't think that he would jump on her, but rather to her surprise she found herself wondering just how she would react if he did.

She went out of the stage door and walked around the theatre offices. She caught a glimpse of the party across the road through the restaurant windows and didn't feel the least inclination to go in. She hurried away towards the car park.

It was completely dark. Lights were on in the main car park by the theatre, but the strip of land by the football pitch was fenced in and immune to any stray spillage. Once she had passed the gap in the fence she had nothing to guide her but faint moonlight, which was barely enough for her to make out the shapes of the cars, let alone identify them. Treading carefully over the uneven, rutted ground, she headed towards where she thought she'd left her Citroën, arms extended as if playing blind man's buff. Her fingers touched the bonnet and she felt her way round to the driver's door, but after a minute of fruitless fumbling with the key she was forced to conclude that it was the wrong car. She was just wondering what to do next when she heard somebody sneeze.

It was a muffled sneeze, not a loud sound, but nonetheless it had come from very near. Sally felt the hairs on her nape rise. She stood very still.

'Hello?' she said cautiously.

There was no answer. It was so dark she couldn't even see her hand in front of her face, but she thought she sensed movement on the other side of the car. Was it her

146

imagination, or was someone coming towards her?

'Who's there?'

Someone was there, she wasn't imagining it. She heard a noise, like a heavy footfall on the grass. A black shape seemed to have detached itself from the blackness all around it and was moving slowly round the front of the car. Her hand, resting on the door which she had tried unsuccessfully to open, felt a tremor run through the metal, and at the same instant she heard the angry whisper of a strangled oath.

'Who's that?'

Her own voice was little more than a whisper, though not through choice. She felt the fear, like a lightning rash, spreading from her lungs to her limbs. A cloud had covered the moon, she could see absolutely nothing. A sudden clear thought pierced her brain: if she could not see, then nor could she be seen.

'Where are you?' said the whispered voice, from so close by she gasped.

There was a sound like paper tearing and a match flared in the darkness. She saw a featureless blur of pale flesh turn towards her, a hand reach out across the narrow space between them. The outstretched fingers brushed her hair, just as the match went out.

She turned and ran blindly through the darkness. It was a miracle she didn't trip on the uneven ground or fall into a car. She might have crashed at full tilt into the fence, but luckily she guessed where the gap was and ran out on to the grass at the back of the theatre. She could see a little light now and she ran gratefully towards it, not daring to look behind her. She tore round the corner of the office building and almost ran straight into the arms of Philip Fletcher.

'What's the hurry?' he asked with a smile, but then he saw her face and became serious. 'What's the matter?'

Her grip round his neck was so tight that he had to

147

gently prise her fingers apart. She was so out of breath she could hardly speak.

'There was someone in the car park . . . It might sound silly but it's so dark . . . I couldn't even find my car.'

'It doesn't sound silly at all. Wait here.'

Philip walked briskly back to the stage door. He returned a few moments later with a uniformed security guard, who was nodding as Philip explained the situation. The guard unclipped a heavy-duty rubber torch from his belt.

'I'm not surprised you couldn't find your car, miss,' said the guard. 'It's pitch black out there. Come with me.'

Sally followed the reassuring bright beam of the torch. Philip came too, though she begged him half-heartedly not to trouble himself further.

'No trouble at all,' he insisted.

She was glad to have both men with her. She clung to Philip's arm as the guard walked down the row of parked cars, pointing his torch between them. No one was there. Philip saw her to her car, which wasn't at all where she had thought she'd left it.

'Will you be all right now?' he asked.

'Yes. Thank you so much, you've been very sweet. Are you going to the party now?'

'No, I've changed my mind. I'm going to call a cab.'

'No need. I'll run you home.'

'Well, if you're sure . . .'

It was only a token protest. She unlocked the passenger door and he climbed in. They waved goodnight to the guard, who they passed on their way out of the car park.

They were both silent. She was aware of his eyes on her and she became self-conscious. Her grip on the wheel was tight and she was hunched awkwardly over it. She tried to relax.

'Left here?' she asked at the roundabout, her voice tight with tension.

'Yes. Then it's to the right after about three-quarters of a mile.'

There were no other cars about, which was probably just as well; she was driving very fast. She forced herself to take her foot off the accelerator, slowed down to a more sensible fifty. They crossed the bridge where Philip had seen her in Dick's car on the first day. She remembered how embarrassed she'd been and involuntarily put her foot to the floor again. She almost missed the turning on the right.

'It's just coming up,' he said another hundred yards further on. 'You can drop me at the top of the drive, there's no need to –'

'No, please. Might as well take you all the way.'

She drove slowly up the long curving drive. She could believe that the house was as impressive as he described it.

'You'll have to see it by daylight,' he said. 'Here we are.'

She pulled up in a big empty courtyard, stopping as instructed next to an exterior stone staircase.

'My flat's on the top floor,' Philip explained genially. 'Thanks very much for the ride. I don't suppose . . .'

He had opened his door, just a fraction but enough for the interior light to come on. Immediately his voice trailed away. Once more she felt him staring at her.

'Sally, are you all right?'

She didn't answer. She couldn't talk to him and nor could she look at him. She stared straight ahead, feeling bewildered, and embarrassed, and utterly wretched. She felt the tears pouring down her cheeks.

'No,' she said simply.

She let him put his arms round her, she was grateful for his shoulder to cry on. She was grateful too that he didn't say anything. There was no point in feeling embarrassed now, she had let herself go too far for that. She didn't try to stop the tears, but let them flow. When he judged that she was finished he gave her a handkerchief.

'Why don't you come inside,' he said gently. 'I'll make you some coffee.'

She nodded. Part of her wanted just to burrow into a corner somewhere and hide, but another part dreaded to be alone. It was ironic that she should let herself go in front of Philip, of all people, but he was being kind, and patient, and he was there. She got out of the car and followed him up the stone staircase. A security light came on automatically and showed the way.

He ushered her into his living room and went next door to put the kettle on. He came back and stood in the doorway, waiting for it to boil.

'Are you comfortable there?' he asked.

There was an armchair and a sofa, but she had chosen instead to sit on one of the hard chairs by the table.

'I'm fine, thanks. God, I must look a mess.'

'You don't. But if you want the bathroom it's down the corridor, first on the right.'

She went to the bathroom while he returned to the kitchen. She washed and saw to her make-up. When she came back he was coming out of the kitchen with a tray. They both sat down at the table.

'Nice flat,' she said.

'I've stayed in worse. Milk or sugar?'

She shook her head. He handed her a mug of black coffee from the tray. He hadn't made one for himself.

'Look, Philip, I'm sorry to do this to you. I hardly even know you, it's most unfair.'

'There's no need to apologize, Sally. You had a nasty experience tonight. I don't know who or what you saw in the car park, but I know you saw something.'

'I'm glad you believe me. I felt a bit foolish when we went back and there was no one there.'

'Of course I believe you. It was obvious from your face something unpleasant had happened. If there was anyone hanging around, a mugger or worse, he'd have had plenty of time to scarper when he saw us coming back with the guard. I know these things aren't supposed to go on in a place like Chichester, but frankly nowhere's safe these days. Look what happened to Dick.'

'I know. I'm a bit on edge tonight. I haven't been having the best of times recently.'

'Do you want to talk about it?'

'I don't want to bore you.'

'You won't, but it's up to you. Look, I'm going to open a bottle of rather good claret I've been saving. I hope, incidentally, you'll join me in a glass, but whether you do or you don't I've no intention of going to bed until the bottle is drunk; to do so would be criminal. Anyway, the point is that I shall be up for at least an hour or so and you're welcome to stay as long as you like. If you want to talk about the production, the theatre in general, or just the weather or the common agricultural policy, that's fine by me, I'm happy to discuss anything you want. But if instead you feel a need to get things off your chest, I'm just as happy to sit and lend a sympathetic ear. It's up to you. Anyway, think about it while I try and remember where I put the corkscrew.'

It didn't take him long to find it. He uncorked the bottle and poured most of it into two of the biggest wine glasses she had ever seen. She pushed aside her barely touched coffee. It was no competition.

She told him about Jason; not everything, but enough. She explained why she'd remained in the theatre after the show and spared no detail in recounting the angry message recorded on her answerphone. She told him about the burglary, about the desecrated photographs, about how the police had naturally suspected Jason. She described the anonymous calls that had plagued her for three months, how even now her heart skipped a beat every time she heard a phone ring. She had thought it might be starting again tonight, but it had only been her flatmate making a bad connection. That was the trouble when something like this happened: paranoia ruled. She told him about the face she had seen hovering above the swimming pool. It probably hadn't been anything sinister, just a kid as Dick had suggested, but it had spooked her, like the incident in the car park tonight. She'd been living on her nerves for too long, bottling it all up inside her, hoping it would all go away. It wouldn't of course. She had bad dreams almost every night.

'You have been in the wars,' he commented when she had finished. 'It can't have been nice having to witness Dick get beaten up.'

'It wasn't. But at least that had nothing to do with me. Or does that sound awful?'

'No, no. It was probably just a discriminating theatre fan exercising his critical faculties. Now *that* does sound awful.'

She laughed. His tone was knowing and playful. It was impossible not to admire his perfect light delivery.

'You two really don't like each other very much, do you?'

'We loathe each other. Utterly.'

'Don't be shy about expressing your feelings now, will you?'

'I shan't.'

She prompted him to give his side of the story, but he really didn't want to discuss Dick Jones. Instead they talked about the play, and about *Antony and Cleopatra*, and mutual friends and acquaintances, both the quick and the dead. He talked at length about Seymour Loseby, sadly deceased, and made her laugh till her ribs ached with his risqué stories. Then he told her about Olive. She was flabbergasted to learn that he too had been harassed. He read to her from the letters and offered as exhibit A the pair of outsize knickers he'd received in the post. She inspected the crotchless material minutely.

'You are full of surprises.'

'I was thinking of having them made into a tea cosy. On second thoughts, two tea cosies. Your glass is empty. Fortunately I have another bottle.'

In fact he had a whole rack of them. He opened two more and they drank them pretty much at the rate of one an hour. She only realized that later, when she chanced to glance at her watch and saw that it was coming up to three o'clock. She hadn't noticed the time fly by. It had been the nicest evening she'd had all year.

'I'd really better be going,' she said. 'We've got two shows tomorrow.'

'You've had quite a lot to drink, Sally. Are you sure you're fit to drive?'

'It's not far.'

'There's a spare bedroom here. I think you should stay.'

'But I don't want to put you to any troub –'

'It's no trouble at all. The bed's made up. You said you weren't going to sleep anyway. You might as well enjoy the wine.'

She hesitated. He'd drunk more than her, it was true, but she must have accounted for at least a bottle. She didn't feel drunk, but she knew she didn't have a chance in hell of passing a breathalyser. Still she hesitated. Her alcoholic intake wasn't the only consideration.

'I trust you are not fearful for your virtue,' he said, as if reading her thoughts. His voice was fruity and theatrical, and not a little slurred. 'Alas, I have imbibed too much myself; the very suggestion is impractical. Egad, fie and upon my word, madam, your reputation is safe with me. And now I think I'd better get to bed myself, before I pass out.'

She ended up having to support him as they made their way down the corridor. He wanted her to have his bed, which he swore was incredibly comfortable, but she insisted very firmly on the spare room. She gave him a goodnight peck on the cheek and went into the bathroom. When she came out again she heard Philip's gentle snores.

She did sleep in the end, though only after dawn and for a few hours. Her sleep was fitful and light, and disturbed by incoherent dreams. One image in particular haunted her. It was of a face, threatening but indistinct, the blurred features changing and rippling moment by moment, as if reflected in water, or lit by a flickering match.

11

When Sally came into the kitchen on Saturday morning she had to laugh. Philip looked even worse than she felt.

'It was the third bottle, I'm afraid,' he said thickly from his position by the kettle, as he concentrated with immense effort on getting the lid off the coffee jar. 'Never did know when to stop . . . you couldn't do this for me, could you?'

He handed her the coffee jar with an expression of weary resignation. After a prolonged struggle Sally succeeded in wrestling off the lid. Philip had rather more success with a box of Nurofen, from which he distributed liberally.

'Sorry it's only instant,' he apologized. 'I'm out of the real stuff. Out of bread and cereal too. Not much use as a host, I'm afraid. I can offer you a bath if you like.'

She declined, for which he must have been grateful; he looked like he needed it more. Both of them were dressed, but he looked suspiciously like he had slept in his clothes; his shirt was almost as creased as his face. His short unkempt hair had the consistency of a flattened doormat.

'I'll go home and take a shower,' she said. 'Think I'll use my landlady's swimming pool first. Might wake me up.'

'Good idea.'

'It would also probably be a good idea if we both got an early night tonight. Do you mind if I pass on dinner?'

'Of course not. Are you around tomorrow?'

'I think so.'

'Well let's see how we both feel tomorrow then. And let's try and concentrate on getting through today. Do we really have two shows? Please tell me I'm only dreaming it.'

'You're not, I'm afraid. The matinee's at three.'

'Oh, bugger.'

He looked as if he had been trying to summon up a more graphic expletive, but the effort defeated him. He set his jaw grimly and muttered something about it being one of those days. She knew what he meant.

She drank her coffee, thanked him profusely for last night's private party and the loan of the bed, and headed out of the flat and down the stone staircase with a lighter step and a jauntier air than seemed to Philip either credible or appropriate. He watched her getting into her car from the kitchen window. Jennifer, out in the courtyard empty-ing the bin, watched her too. When Sally had driven off, his landlady went back inside wearing a studiedly humourless expression. Philip sighed and went to run a bath. It was all very well being hung for a sheep as for a lamb, but he was in danger of being condemned for bugger all.

He lay in the bath immersed to the chin, dozing fitfully and listening to the radio for the best part of an hour. It didn't do much for the creased look of his skin, but as his headache receded he did begin to feel almost human again. Sally had been correct to surmise that he had slept in his clothes. He had fallen on to the bed and passed out in one continuous motion. He supposed he must have been horribly smashed. His recollection of the previous night was none too clear.

'Did she really sleep next door to me entirely un-molested?' he wondered aloud. 'I'm either losing my touch or getting soft in my old age. I don't know which

156

is worse. Some consolation, though: I couldn't have been more wrong about her and Jones.'

He felt some embarrassment as he recalled his petulant behaviour during rehearsals. He shivered, and not on account of the rapidly cooling water: God, but he made himself cringe sometimes! He could see now that Dick had been winding him up, wanting him to think that there was as much going on as met the eye, and of course he had succeeded; Philip had fallen hook, line and the other thing . . . But gossip in the company, in particular a source of information he had always regarded as beyond reproach, had also contributed to his misapprehension. He hoped it wasn't too late to make good the error. Sally Blair was, not to put too fine a point on it, utterly drop-dead gorgeous.

Eventually he rose from the bath, dressed in fresh clothes and contemplated the rest of the day with negative enthusiasm. It was half past ten. There being nothing in the house he supposed that he should set off in search of breakfast. He supposed, too, that as this would mean walking past the newsagent's on the way to town he would be duty bound to check whether or not the notices were in. The prospect failed to appeal. He steeled himself for his walk by grimly mouthing the conviction that it would do him good.

As it turned out he wasn't kidding himself; his first step out into the fresh air revived him. It was a cool day, he took deep breaths and felt the crisp oxygen scour his lungs, the blood flow again through his sluggish veins. Even before he'd reached the end of the drive he had walked off the residue of his headache and much of the stiffness in his limbs. He set off towards town with something approaching an optimistic gait.

So, the show last night hadn't gone strictly according to plan. Well, what of that? he asked himself. He'd known worse, and a critic would have to have been in a particularly savage mood not to acknowledge that at the least the production (and P. Fletcher's performance) was solidly competent. It had been much better than that, of course, and toupee trouble notwithstanding the more percipient critics would undoubtedly acknowledge the fact. He didn't think that any damage could have been done to his reputation – no, the foundations were much too secure. Sadly, but realistically, there weren't going to be any rave reviews, but he'd never truly believed all the transfer talk anyway (it was an expensive show to take into the West End) so he didn't think anything had been actually lost – except the chance to outshine Jones. It was a complicated equation, of course, there were so many different factors to consider . . .

He slowed down as he approached the narrow stone bridge. He was half muttering his thoughts as he walked, sorting them into order, but he had become dimly aware of a car approaching from behind. The bridge had no pavement and it would be safer to let it pass. He stopped at the side of the road and carried on vaguely thinking aloud.

'Probably get a short tour out of it, six or eight weeks . . . plenty of time to get something lined up for the autumn . . . could do with a well-paid telly . . . who've we got coming up here then? Stirling Moss?'

The car was shooting towards him at top speed; the engine buzzed and hummed like an angry wasp. The vehicle seemed to be only half on the road. The offside wheels were scratching up clouds of dust in the verge. Philip glanced anxiously back towards the bridge. There didn't seem to be anything coming the other way, which was just as well: in that confined space there must have been a collision. He was glad he had decided to wait before walking over.

A sharp cracking noise made him turn back. He was in time to see two parts of a thick twig fly out from beneath the tyres of the car, which now seemed to be hardly on the road at all. Philip stared at it in amazement. It was a matter of yards away and it was coming straight for him. He threw himself backwards without looking.

He fell heavily on to stony ground as the car flashed by in a white blur. He was too stunned to notice anything; he didn't even catch a glimpse of the driver. His fall had knocked the breath out of him. He lay winded and stinging with the roar of the engine still ringing in his ears.

He was stinging because he had fallen into a bed of nettles. His left hand and wrist were covered in red splotches. It was the pain that cut through the numbness in his brain and started him back into action.

He stumbled to his feet and ran out into the middle of the bridge. Unfortunately he wasn't quick enough. The car was a dot in the distance now, too far away for him to be able to read the number. All he could tell was the colour, white. He swore at it and gestured furiously.

He was trembling all over as he went in search of some dock leaves. He found some and stared in disbelief at his hand before rubbing them in. He could scarcely believe what had just happened; the eruptions on his skin were a necessary proof. He had come within a whisker of being killed, almost literally. He felt sick.

He had to sit down for a moment; he repaired to a tree and crouched against it. He had had some close shaves in his time. He had been shot at and badly beaten; for years he had flirted brazenly with death and violence. His nerves had been stretched to breaking point more times than he could remember, but he'd never felt as bad as this. A snort of incredulity escaped him: to have been through all he had been through and then nearly to succumb to some ridiculous trivial accident! He might have found the irony droll had he not been so incandescent with rage.

He had still not calmed down by the time he reached the theatre, a slow painful ten minutes later. He'd forgotten about breakfast, he'd even forgotten about the reviews. Thankfully there was no one about to engage him in conversation. He thought about calling the police, but decided there was no point. He collected his key, made a disgusting cup of coffee in the crew room on the way, then locked himself away.

He lay on his couch listlessly for the next couple of hours, occasionally rubbing the dock leaves into his sore skin, to no apparent benefit, and trying in vain to banish grim intimations of mortality. He noticed that he had a touch of the shakes as he undressed and began to get into costume. He attributed them to his alcoholic binge of the previous night.

Around lunchtime the corridors backstage began to come alive. The actors arrived in dribs and drabs, running the gauntlet of autograph hunters at the stage door, always at their thickest on a matinee day. Most gathered in the Green Room for food and drink. Sally, who had eaten at home, turned up as late as possible and went directly to her dressing room. Although her hangover had passed she felt low on energy and wasn't in a convivial mood. The thought of having to do two shows filled her with dread.

She wasn't alone. When she popped out to get a drink just before the half she caught a glimpse of Philip through his dressing-room door, sitting in his waistcoat and breeches and staring dully into his own reflection in the mirror. His dresser was putting on his wig.

'You look like death warmed up,' Sally remarked lightly.

He could hardly even muster a smile in reply. The wig was just going on, he couldn't turn to look at her. The dresser carefully patted down the lace strips at his temples, which glistened with glue.

'What have you got to be cheerful about?' Philip demanded expressionlessly. 'You obviously haven't seen the notices.'

'No I haven't.' Sally swallowed. 'Tell me the worst.'

'Actually they're not so bad. Allegedly. I haven't seen

them myself, but Dawn tells me they're okay. *Telegraph* actually quite nice. *Independent* a bit indifferent. Those the only two so far. Neither actually mentions you-know-what as such. Unaccustomedly decent of them. There, that should do the bugger . . .'

He was referring to the wig. He turned his head from side to side, examining it critically in profile.

'Used practically a whole pot of gum. If that doesn't stick it I'll incinerate the bloody thing.'

'Well do let us know in good time. We'll have a barbecue.'

She walked on down the corridor to the crew room. Robert Hammond was just filling the kettle.

'Sally! Where did you get to last night?'

'Oh, I'm sorry. I wasn't feeling well.'

'I heard you got spooked in the car park.'

'Who told you that?'

'One of the security people. I went looking for you, he was at the stage door, told me he'd just showed you to your car. I must have missed you by a couple of minutes.'

'Robert, that's very sweet of you. Did I miss a great party?'

'No.'

They both laughed. Robert gave her a brief résumé of the party highlights, which didn't take long. Apparently Julian had fallen in love with one of the waiters and Roy had drunk enough to fill a camel.

'Was he even more obnoxious than usual?' Sally wanted to know.

'Impossible to tell. At least he didn't bore anyone by talking to them. He was too busy eating. Are you feeling better today?'

'Oh, as well as can be expected facing up to the prospect of two shows.'

'If you manage to survive them I hope you'll allow me to buy you a drink afterwards.'

'No, no, let me buy you one.'

Before they could launch into a full-scale argument the tannoy announced the half-hour call. They agreed to suspend their disagreement until later.

In the meantime they had the little matter of the first show to negotiate. Second nights in the theatre are always notoriously flat, and it didn't help that this was an afternoon and not an evening performance. Everyone was anxious to get the production back on the rails as smoothly as possible, and there was something of a siege mentality backstage.

They got off to a flying start. The audience was a near full-house and made it clear almost from the opening lines that they were there strictly to enjoy themselves. The first half went without a hitch, but of course it was what lay ahead after the interval that preyed on their minds. In the event they needn't have worried. There was a perceptible tightening of tension at the commencement of *that* scene, but the fatal moment came and passed without mishap and the laughter never fluctuated. Afterwards the actors pretended to have been feeling relaxed about it all along, protesting that *of course* lightning never struck twice, but the palpable relief on everyone's faces rather gave the lie to the general affectation. The rest of the play was a case of downhill all the way, in the best of senses, with the laughter snowballing from scene to scene. At the end the cast took four curtain calls with some sections of the audience standing to applaud.

The reaction was gratifying, but there was no time for them to rest on their laurels. They had just over an hour between curtain down and the half for the evening show. Sally had just finished changing out of her costume, with Martha's help, when there was a tannoy message to tell her that she had a visitor waiting at stage door.

She was going that way anyway, planning to avoid last night's mistake and move her car round in good time, but

162

when she got to the stage door there was no one there.

'He was here a moment ago,' said the stage doorkeeper, sticking her head out of her cubbyhole and looking around. 'He didn't come up to you, did he?'

He hadn't. Nor, it transpired, had he left a name. Sally wasn't expecting any visitors. She went outside cautiously, thinking of familiar faces she would prefer not to see.

There were none amongst the autograph hunters who pounced on her. Some had caught her on the way in, but there never seemed to be any shortage of fans desperate for her signature. Their tenacity amazed her. They were always there come rain or shine, often for hours at a time. The Chichester fans, as befitted the audiences, may have been unusually elderly, but they were just as keen, and just as particular, as fans anywhere else. It rarely sufficed for her just to sign her name anyhow or anywhere: oh no, there were special pages in special albums, or strictly designated parts of the programme, or sometimes photographs or articles taken from magazines that had to be specifically inscribed. Dedications were frequently demanded, and it was an inviolable rule that wherever possible the name of the collector should boast the most obscure spelling variant possible. Sally was always being made to feel as if she were on the verge of causing some catastrophic diplomatic incident.

Her duty done and a good five minutes of her precious break wasted she pulled away, leaving the unsated pack sniffing hungrily for fresh blood. They would have a thin time of it, since most of the actors would be in the Green Room. She intended to join them as soon as possible. She set off rapidly towards the car park. As she rounded the offices she became aware of someone approaching rapidly from behind. She glanced back over her shoulder. When she saw who it was she stopped walking.

'Where are you going in such a hurry?' he demanded belligerently. 'Afraid of me, are you?'

She took her time before replying. She wanted to sound calm.

'I didn't know it was you. You didn't leave a name.'

'If I'd left my name you'd have run a mile. Why didn't you ring?'

His voice had always sounded like a high-pitched whine when he was angry. He was angry now. His thin lips quivered and his watery blue eyes flashed ominously. The last of the audience was still leaving the theatre, she was aware of people glancing across. She didn't want to be having this scene in the first place, and certainly not in public.

'Why didn't you ring?' he repeated obstinately. 'I left you a number.'

'Jason, please calm down.'

She knew at once it was the wrong thing to have said, but then wasn't it always? His long pale face went even whiter, the usual sign prior to an eruption. When it came it was surprisingly controlled.

'Calm? You want me to be fucking calm? Oh that's just fucking peachy!'

He may not have shouted but his diction was clear enough to reach the ears of passers-by. The barrage of scandalized looks which he now received, and to which he was oblivious, were of the kind usually reserved for reaction to onstage nudity, not that there was ever much of that down Chichester way.

'Jason, I don't think –'

'You know I've just driven here all the way from Birmingham. That's three fucking hours, you know that, and for what? For you to tell me to calm down! All I wanted was that you give me a ring; I left you a number, it wasn't too much to ask, was it?'

'I only got the message last night.'

'Then why didn't you ring last night? Or this morning?'

'Jason, please stop talking to me like I'm a war criminal. Look, I'm sorry, I'm sorry for everything, but let's not have a slanging match here. I haven't got much time, but –'

'Oh, you haven't got much time, have you? Oh that's just great, after I've driven for three hours all the way from –'

'Jason, I haven't got any time because I've got another show to do in under an hour. Now shut the fuck up, will you?'

She shouted the words at him. It shut him up, temporarily. It also earned her some extra filthy looks from the passers-by.

'We'll go to my dressing room,' she said, making herself sound calm again. 'I'm just going to bring my car round, all right? I'll be five minutes, why don't you go back and wait for me at the stage door?'

He didn't answer. When she grew tired of waiting for a reply she started walking towards the football pitch. After a moment he followed her.

'I couldn't believe it when the police turned up on my doorstep,' she heard him muttering. 'I thought it was someone's idea of a joke, Jeremy Beadle or –'

'I'm not listening, Jason. We'll talk in my dressing room, all right?'

He mumbled something incoherent but tonally self-pitying. Sally walked faster.

'Why didn't you ring?'

'Look, we'll talk when we're inside.'

'What are you scared of?'

Him, was the answer. She remembered how it felt to have his hands round her throat. It may have been an aberration, and she had thought his remorse as genuine as it was overwhelming, but she didn't want to take any chances. He seemed quite as volatile today as he had been

165

on the night of that terrible, terminal row. Perhaps the sight of her acted as a trigger, unleashing violent passions. She wished fervently that he hadn't followed her out to the car park. She would be able to deal with him more comfortably in her dressing room, on her own territory.

'Am I so frightening, Sally? Am I? I just wanted to talk to you, all you had to do was pick up the phone. I was devastated. You said just now I was talking to you like a criminal, well how do you think I felt? What did you tell the police? They were treating me like some kind of weirdo, giving me the third degree. I didn't make any stupid phone calls to you. I was trying to forget you. I couldn't. I still love you. If that makes me a weirdo, too bad, I can't help it . . .'

His voice cracked. As they reached her car he seemed to crumple. He stood bent over the roof, his face buried in his arms, his body twitching with silent sobs, as she unlocked the door. She felt close to tears herself.

'Look,' she said gently. 'Just go round the other side and get in. Then we'll go back and have a cup of tea –'

He banged on the roof violently with his fist. The suddenness of the blow made her jump.

'Didn't you hear what I said?'

His voice was so strained she could hardly make out the words. He turned his head slowly towards her. His eyes were filled with pain and humiliation, and tears.

'I said I still love you, Sal.'

He lurched towards her. She recoiled instinctively, but not enough. His body pressed her back against the car door.

'I want you back,' he said hoarsely.

Clumsily he tried to kiss her. She turned her face enough to deflect him, but when she tried to raise her hands to push him off he grabbed both her wrists and pinned her.

'Jason, let go.'

166

'It's all right, Sally, I forgive you, I know you didn't mean to hurt me –'

'Jason, you're hurting me –'

'Let her go!' a man's angry voice barked from only a few feet away.

Instinctively Jason released her and they both sprang apart, each as startled as the other. A man was standing on the other side of the car, glaring at them. He was thirtyish, dark, thickset. Though he must have been heavy on his feet neither had heard his approach.

'You keep your filthy hands to yourself,' he snarled. He started to come round the front of the car.

'Sorry, am I missing something or what?' Jason asked with an incredulous snort. 'Just who the fuck are you, mate?'

The man didn't answer him. Instead he came and stood between them. He wasn't big, but Sally felt there was something intimidating about him. It may have been simply the fact that he was wearing mirror sunglasses and she couldn't see his eyes.

'It's going to be all right,' he said to her in an oddly soothing tone. 'I'm going to take good care of you, Sally.'

'You know this wanker, do you?' demanded Jason.

She didn't. She knew she'd never seen this man in her life. She felt cold all over. She had never heard anything so terrifying as her name dropping from this stranger's lips.

'Look, mate, why don't you just –'

Sally screamed. Jason never saw the knife. She saw it, a metal blur that sliced through flesh like the cut of a butcher and made the blood fall in showers across the grass.

12

Philip was in his dressing room talking to Carol the wig mistress when he thought he heard someone screaming.

'What was that?' he asked, breaking off their polite but intensely confrontational argument. She wanted him to take his wig off so that she could clean it; he, on the other hand, was adamant that once on for the matinee it might as well stay on for the evening. By the same token he had not bothered to change out of his costume.

'What was what?' she said.

'That noise. Sounded like it was coming from outside.'

The view from his window was restricted. He pressed his nose to the glass and peered out as well as he could. After giving him a few moments and finding herself none the wiser, Carol resumed the argument.

'Besides anything else, all that gum isn't good for the lace. And it really does need a thorough combing out. Aren't you boiling hot in it?'

'No. Nothing wrong with a bit of wholesome sweat in any – there! you must have heard that!'

'I did.'

She joined him at the window. They both craned their necks in a futile attempt to see round the corner.

'It was definitely a scream,' said Philip.

'Yes. It came from over by the car park. Or perhaps the tennis courts. Could just be people larking about.'

'It sounded too dramatic for that. Where's Jenny going in such a hurry?'

Jenny was tearing across the grass at full speed, her arms and legs flailing. She was tripping and stumbling at every step in a display of rank uncoordination. Philip called out to her.

'Jenny, what's the matter?'

She shouted something back, but her voice was breathless and incoherent. However, the note of panic was unmistakable.

'I think there was something about an ambulance,' said Carol. 'Do you think someone's been hurt?'

'We'd better go and find out.'

They both hurried down to the stage door, the direction in which Jenny had been headed. She burst in yelling at the top of her voice just as they arrived.

'Quick! Call an ambulance! Call police! Help! Car park . . . Sally!'

Her legs gave way and she collapsed into a nervous heap on the floor. Everyone was talking at once: Jenny, Philip, Carol, the stage doorkeeper, even Roy Power, who happened to have just appeared on the scene. Philip shouted for quiet. When the noise had subsided he put on his most masterful air and took control.

'Calm down, everyone!' To Jenny: 'Try and get your breath back, tell us clearly what happened.' To the stage doorkeeper: 'You'd better dial 999, police and ambulance.' To Carol: 'Can you get the first-aid kit? Now Jenny –'

'What do you want me to do?' interrupted Roy Power.

'Shut up. Jenny, are you –'

'I'm only trying to help!' whined Roy. 'There's no need to –'

'Shut the fuck up, Roy!'

Roy looked outraged. He stood glaring at Philip and muttering darkly. Philip turned his back on him.

'Now, Jenny, take your time. What happened?'

'There isn't any time!' she replied desperately. 'He may be bleeding to death.'

'Who?'

'The man who was with Sally. I've never seen him before.'

'Where's Sally?'

'She's been . . .' Jenny's eyes had glazed over; she was numb with shock. She seemed to be having trouble finding the right word. It hit her suddenly: 'She's been kidnapped!'

Carol reappeared with a first-aid kit and Robert and Julian in tow. Philip gave a general rallying cry.

'To the car park, everyone. No time to lose!'

They all burst out of the stage door together in a tight-knit pack, scattering the startled autograph hunters like so much chaff. With a plaintive chorus of requests for their signatures ringing in their ears they sprinted for the car park. Jenny did her breathless best to fill in Philip on the way.

He gathered that she had been going to move her car, that just as she had come round the corner she had seen Sally and a tall fair young man in heated conversation; that another, darker man had appeared at that moment, that the fair man had shouted at him, that the darker man had produced a knife, and then –

He could see the rest for himself. They gathered round the fair young man in silent horror. His white shirt, his whiter face and the grass all around were drenched with blood.

'Good God!' exclaimed Julian. 'It's Jason Barrington. I worked with him in Leeds.'

He knelt and felt for a pulse.

'He's alive!'

They ripped open the first-aid kit frantically. Julian and Carol seemed to know what they were doing. Philip left them to tend to Jason while he took Jenny to one side.

'Now what happened to Sally?'

'The other man dragged her away. She was screaming and struggling but he had his arms round her throat. He bundled her into the back of his van and drove off.'

'Did you see the registration?' asked Robert, who had come up to join them.

'Sorry, no, it happened too quickly.'

'What colour was the van?'

'White.'

'White?'

'What did the man look like?' demanded Philip.

'Er, not too tall, but quite big, you know what I mean? God, I can't think . . . dressed in jeans, black T-shirt. Didn't see his face. He was wearing sunglasses.'

Robert looked thoughtful.

'It could just be coincidence, but Sally said the guy who beat up Dick had a white van. I'm going to go and see if there's anyone around who might have seen something.'

He raced off towards the car park exit.

'Give me a hand, please,' said Julian.

Philip helped Carol hold up Jason while Julian looped bandages round his chest and shoulders.

'Is he going to be all right?' asked Philip.

'Three deep cuts, but it's not as bad as it looks. Lost a lot of blood though, hope the ambulance gets here soon.'

'And the police,' added Philip, rather taking himself by surprise. He had never thought that he might someday be in a position where he would be glad to see them.

'Will they know where to come?' asked Carol.

'I don't know. I'll go and make sure. You'll be all right here?'

'Fine.'

Philip started running back towards the theatre. As he approached the offices he slowed down, giving his thoughts time to catch up.

Could it have been a van that had almost knocked him

down that morning? He hadn't seen what kind of vehicle it was, he had just noted the colour – the same colour as the van Sally had seen at the restaurant, the same –

'Philip?'

He turned distractedly at the sound of Jenny's voice. She was running across the grass after him. The knifeman had been dressed in black and wore sunglasses. The man he'd seen at the cricket match, the startled photographer, fitted the same description. He'd shouted out something cryptic as he ran off. As he ran towards his white van.

'Philip, they said to ask for some blankets.'

'Yes, of course . . .'

He walked on, immersed in his own thoughts. He'd seen the man at the cricket match while he was looking for Olive. They must have both gone off in the same direction. The coincidences were piling up. He remembered how he'd heard a car arrive just as he was about to leave Olive's farm. Only it hadn't been a car, it had been a white van.

'Christ! I've got to ring the police!'

He broke into a run again, leaving Jenny trailing behind. She was shouting something at him, but he wasn't listening. A terrible panic had seized him, blotting out everything from his mind save the outsize image of Olive and the desperate intensity he had seen in her face the other night. Why had he been so sure that her obsession was benign? The woman was clearly a fanatic, probably deranged; how could anyone begin to second-guess what was going on in her weird, sick brain? What a bloody fool he'd been! This dark man, the van driver, had to be her accomplice, perhaps even her lover. What sort of lunatic schemes had the two of them concocted together? A horrible thought, worse even than all the others, imploded suddenly inside his head: what if it had been the dark man in the car park last night, spooking Sally? What if he'd followed them home, reported back to Olive that they seemed to have spent the night together? To Olive's

172

twisted way of thinking that would amount to a betrayal. She may have instructed the van driver to frighten him, or worse, that morning. And now she could be about to inflict some terrible revenge on Sally, to punish her. It was such a ludicrous notion he was almost convinced it had to be true.

He raced around the corner and into the pack of autograph hunters for the second time, but this time they hardly paid him any attention. They were all eagerly clustering around Dick Jones.

Dick was just parking his red BMW in one of the reserved spaces outside the stage door, making a great show of handling the car deftly despite his bandaged arm. The autograph hunters were buzzing him like flies round a manure heap.

'Nobody told me there was a fancy dress party tonight!' he quipped when he caught sight of Philip in his costume. He opened the car door and took on the painful task of climbing out with conspicuous bravery.

'Philip!' called Jenny, catching up with him at last and thrusting a mobile phone into his hand. 'Here, use this.'

'Thanks . . .'

He hesitated for a fraction of a second. It seemed like ages since the stage door had rung 999, but there were no sirens rending the air. If he rang them now, how long would they take to get to Heron Farm? He could be there in five minutes.

'Dick, give me your car keys!'

Dick was signing his name. He paid Philip no attention.

'Do you think I could have yours, Mr Fletcher?' asked a fringe member of the hunting party who had shrewdly realized that it would be a few minutes or more before he could get to the main quarry. He gave a little snicker as he extended his album and pen: 'Seeing as you're here . . .'

Philip stared for a second at the little open book and the neat blank pages facing him, and at the equally neat

173

blank face of its owner. How many facile insincere grins had he exchanged at stage doors up and down the country during his working life? How many hours had he wasted scrawling his name for the various acolytes of this conspiracy of nerds?

'Oh get a life!' he sighed, and sent the book and pen flying with a flick of the wrist. He put his head down and barged aggressively through the small crowd, elbows first, until he was face to face with Dick Jones.

'Dick, give me your car keys. Now!'

'What the hell's the matter with you, Fletcher? Have you gone stark raving mad?'

Dick was wearing a light summer jacket. Philip thrust his hands simultaneously into the two side pockets.

'What the . . .'

There was a key ring in each pocket. Philip snatched them both, clocked the one with a BMW fob and dropped the other. He grabbed at the car door.

Dick seized him by the sleeve. The grip was strong and Philip couldn't help but give a little malicious chuckle when he saw that it had been made with the bandaged hand.

'Let go of my arm, Dick, this is an emergency.'

'I'm warning you, Fletcher, give me those keys back now or else –'

Philip punched Dick bang in the middle of his nose. Dick staggered back, tripped over his own feet and fell to the ground.

'Or else what?' Philip enquired.

A camera clicked. Christmas had come early for one of the autograph hunters. He stood snapping alternately at Dick, trying to staunch the flow of blood from his nose with a tissue, and Philip, trying to find the ignition and start the car. Philip succeeded first. The car jerked forward about three feet, then stalled.

'Get yourself an automatic next time, Dick.'

Philip restarted the car. Dick pulled himself up on to his knees and shook his bloody tissue at him.

'I'll have your guts for garters, Fletcher! Assault! Theft! I'll sue you for every penny –'

'Ha ha, Dick,' said Philip and put his foot to the floor.

The car accelerated from a standing start at tremendous speed. Philip almost crashed straight into the kerb opposite. He managed to spin the steering wheel round in time, though not before the car had slewed a couple of feet sideways, causing some unfortunate pedestrians to gasp in terror. At least Philip supposed it had been out of terror, though it was possible that it might simply have been out of amazement at the sight of him driving in wig and period costume. The drivers of the cars he now passed were giving him similarly astonished looks, though he realized when he got to the end of the theatre slip-road that it may have been merely on account of his having been going in the wrong direction along a one-way route. He shrugged to himself as he raced out on to the main road. He really didn't have time to observe the niceties of highway protocol.

He overtook everything he met recklessly, the needle on the speedometer hovering most of the way between eighty and ninety. He'd never driven this fast before, but then he'd never driven much anyway. He had no time for cars, he'd never owned one, and though he'd taken his test years ago for professional purposes he had very little idea of what he was doing. The other road-users may have deduced as much. At any rate they seemed to be keen to flash their lights and sound their horns at him. He had no idea where his own light switches were located, but he answered with his horn vigorously.

A mile from the theatre he passed a junction that led to his digs. He'd come that way the other night, emerging where he was now on to the main road and cycling the rest of the way to Goodwood down progressively narrower

175

lanes. He almost overshot his turning but braked just in time. Nonetheless he took out a hefty slice of hedge before careering into the first tight corner blindly. Fortunately nothing was coming the other way.

He didn't let up, but trusted to luck and drove as fast as he could. Who knew what terrifying schemes the mad Olive and her black-clad accomplice might have concocted? Sally would be at their mercy, and he'd seen with his own eyes what that entailed. The blood-boltered torso of her friend in the car park was vivid in his imagination. He put his foot down even harder.

He had to slow up a minute later when he came to the turning with the farm signpost. On his right was the gate where he'd left his bicycle, and beyond that the field across which he'd walked. He'd driven thus far on impulse, but now he was approaching the farm he began belatedly to wonder exactly what he was going to do. Would there be just the two of them, or might there be a gang? Would Olive have a knife too, or a gun? It was hardly as if he was equipped to deal with either eventuality. He wasn't even wearing his sword, the one item of his costume which might have been of any use. He'd left in such a hurry he hadn't thought to tell anyone where he was going.

He noticed Jenny's mobile phone. It was lying on the passenger seat, he must have thrown it there when he jumped in, though he had no recollection of so doing. He snatched it up, clumsily dialled 999 with one hand while controlling the car with the other. He pressed his ear to the receiver but heard nothing. Had it connected? He was about to try again when he rounded a bend and found himself directly outside the muddy drive that led up to the farm. He braked and swung the car into it, almost losing control. He dropped the phone, grabbed the wheel with both hands, and saw too late that another vehicle was only yards away and coming up the drive straight at him. He braked again, instinctively, and desperately tried to aim the BMW away.

The oncoming vehicle smacked into his rear passenger side. The back of the car spun through a hundred and eighty degrees and only stopped spinning because it hit a tree. Philip felt himself being yanked out from behind the wheel.

Should have put the seat belt on, he had time to think, as he was flung sideways across the handbrake. He threw up his hands protectively but barely cushioned the impact as he fell headlong against the door. Either the car was still spinning or his head was corkscrewing into his shoulders like a child's top. He tried to pull himself up, but he was so disoriented he had no idea which way was up. Somehow he managed to tumble out of the car, but he promptly fell on to his head. After a moment of flailing about like a landed fish, he passed out.

He did not feel the strong hands that pulled him off the ground by the lapels, hoisted him in a fireman's lift and carried him back down the muddy drive towards the farmhouse.

13

It was a big room, but the low ceiling made it feel small. The curtains in the tiny windows were drawn, further adding to a sense of claustrophobia, though the stream of light from the open-plan kitchen could not be blocked. The tantalizing glimpse of trees and a yellow field through the glass back door glowed like a beacon in the confined unlit space inside.

There was one other source of light. The television was on in the corner, though the volume was set so low as to be almost inaudible. The VCR panel glowed, showing that a tape was running. The show on TV was the last episode of *Paramedics*.

Sally watched herself dying on screen. No one was supposed to know whether she had actually died or not, it was meant to be a cliffhanger to keep the audience guessing till the second series, but the story had been leaked, to the fury of the producers. In the ensuing furore, blown as usual out of all proportion in the tabloid media pages, Sally must have seemed like the only person in the world who didn't care. She didn't. She'd hated every minute of making *Paramedics*, a show so cheap and tacky that it made the production values of Australian soaps look like *Brideshead Revisited*. Filming her death scene had been one of the happiest experiences of her life.

She heard the man coughing in the next room. She felt her scalp tingle, a sick leaden stirring in the pit of her stomach. She presumed from the sound of running water that the man was in the bathroom, probably washing the blood from his arms and face. A thick green velvet curtain covered the entrance to the hallway. If she craned her neck she could just see the foot of a staircase through a crack in the middle. She had tried to move her chair back, to get a better view, but she couldn't get sufficient purchase.

Her ankles were tied securely to the legs of the chair. She could hardly move her feet. Her wrists were bound together through one of the slats in the back of the chair. She could at least move her arms up and down a little, though not to any purpose. The ropes hurt. She had cried out when he was tying the knots, but he had gritted his teeth and tied them harder. *It's your own fault*, she had heard him mutter when he was behind her, fastening her hands, *it's your own fault, Sally . . .*

She had stopped struggling by then. She had fought when he had forced her into the back of the van, and when she'd found the back doors locked she'd tried to scramble into the front while they were on the move, to escape through the passenger door. He had grabbed her by the neck, held her face down between the two seats while he drove one-handed the rest of the way. She had realized then just how strong he was. Fortunately it had not been a long drive. When they stopped and he came round to unlock the back she had come out running and so taken him by surprise that she'd gained herself a good few yards' start. She'd seen the roof of a big house through the trees and she'd made directly for it. She was no slouch, she'd been a good athlete at school, but her sandals were useless for speed, she had stubbed her toe painfully against a stone, stumbled and slithered on the muddy path. He'd caught up, and dragged her back to his solitary cottage with his arm choking her throat. Then he had tied her to the chair with ropes taken from the back of the van and disappeared next door.

Mud from her fall was all over the knees of her jeans and the front of her white T-shirt. There were more sinister stains too, irregular spots and flecks of blood, already dry and the colour of bright rust. It made her queasy seeing them, but there was something else that made her feel much, much worse. His angry muttered words were ringing in her head.

It's your own fault, Sally . . .

He knew her name. He'd used it in the car park. She'd wondered then if he'd just chanced to recognize her, but once he'd got her into the cottage she had known that there was more to it than that. The television was already on when they came in. She had not realized what programme was showing until he had gone next door.

Now she was alone and helpless, watching herself die. But there was no blurring between fact and fiction in her perceptions. The reality was the rope cutting into her skin, the bloodstains on her clothes. Nor was it the result of a random act. She had been abducted by a murderous knife-wielding maniac who knew exactly who she was. It was much worse than what was happening on TV.

She heard a door close nearby, and a footstep out in the hall. The green curtain parted and the man came into the room. He didn't look at her. Instead he went and stood in front of the television and watched. In his hand he held a portable cassette recorder.

'Who are you?' Sally asked.

He didn't answer, he merely inclined his head a fraction towards her, to show that he had heard. He hadn't changed, he was wearing the same black jeans and T-shirt. No blood was visible, but there were sweat stains under the arms and at the small of the back. She saw him in three-quarters profile from the back. His mouth and lips

180

were immobile, the eyes invisible behind the mirror sunglasses.

'Look, it doesn't matter who you are,' said Sally, concentrating on keeping her voice steady, trying to sound reasonable and calm. 'Why don't you just untie me, let me go, and I promise not to tell anyone anything about you, no one need know . . . anything at all.'

She could hardly make herself finish the sentence. It sounded so stupid, he must know it as well as she did. As if he would let her go free after what she had seen in the car park! If Jason was dead then this man was a murderer. What had he to lose now, and why should he spare the prosecution's only witness?

'Look, let's try and work this out . . .'

She wondered if she was making it worse by speaking, but then how much worse could it possibly get? She had read about hostage situations, the survivors always said how important it was to make contact with their captors. She had read too about the psychology of certain sorts of murderers, to whom the victim was a characterless thing, not a living person at all. If she kept talking she might get through to him, touch his human core. Whatever she did she mustn't let him see her fear. What if he didn't have a human core? She looked at his blank unresponsive profile. He seemed to have known exactly what he was doing all along. How many other victims had he dragged back to his lair? How many times had he raped and killed?

The TV show had ended, the credits were rolling against the background of her fellow actors passing her lifeless body on a stretcher into a helicopter, the ultimate 'watch this space!' tease. She had an idea.

'I can't tell you the trouble they had with that helicopter shot,' she said, in as amiable and conversational tone as a girl could be expected to manage while trussed up like a chicken. 'They're incredibly expensive to hire, every time we used one it ate up half the budget, but the pilot they sent us that day hadn't got a clue what he was doing, the director just couldn't get the shot he wanted, and our producer was going frantic. In the end we . . . well, you see there was only about twenty minutes of daylight left and . . . and you see, we just had to cheat . . .'

The man gave no sign that he'd taken in a word. As soon as the episode was over he'd ejected the cassette and immediately inserted another. As Sally saw what he was playing now her concentration wavered. It was an episode of *Eastenders*, nearly three years old. She didn't watch *Eastenders*, but she knew every detail of this one: it had been her first ever telly role, she'd had about three lines while she was being chatted up by one of the regulars in the Queen Vic. The man had pressed the fast forward button. He released it exactly on cue, just as her scene was beginning. He turned from the television and came towards her, stopping about three feet away. He put the cassette recorder down on the table.

He put down something else as well, something which he'd had tucked under his arm and which she hadn't noticed in the half-light. It was the red folder which she had last seen in her dressing room the night before, the one containing the production photographs.

She had stopped talking. The words had dried up, even the very thoughts for framing were stillborn in her head. She stared at the red folder. He had been in her dressing room. He was the man Antonia had spoken to. And she had seen him before.

She remembered the outline of a face, no more than an amorphous shape in the headlamps of a white van. The face had turned to her when she had screamed, she had felt those unseen eyes penetrating her, the same sensation she had experienced earlier that day in the swimming pool, the same exactly as she was experiencing now.

'What do you want from me?' she asked, and prayed

that her voice hadn't been as small and thin as it had sounded in her own ears.

He was still standing in front of her. He was shifting his weight a little from foot to foot, he looked awkward, perhaps even abashed. Sally wondered if she dared let her hopes rise. Could this reticence be taken as a sign of latent humanity? The man cleared his throat. He opened the red folder, took out the photograph on top, and pushed it along the table towards her.

'My favourite,' he said, almost too softly for her to catch.

She looked at the photograph. It showed her in her Act III boy's costume, she looked wide-eyed and pretty but faintly androgynous. She knew the photo intimately, a copy was blown up and on display in the foyer. But in the theatre, as in the negative, it showed her and Philip together. Philip wasn't in this print, it was just her on her own. The rest of it had been crudely cut away with scissors.

She opened her mouth wide and screamed with all the power in her lungs. The room reverberated, her ears ached with her own noise. The man recoiled for a moment, then sprang forward, attempting to cover her face with his hand. She bit him deep into his little finger. He struck her across the head.

It was a hard, savage blow, enough to send her crashing sideways to the carpet. There was a splitting sound of wood breaking as the chair hit the floor, then a mighty thud as her head followed. Her eyes went out of focus as the room began twirling round. When she came to again he had lifted the chair back to an upright position and his arms and body were round her in a tense bearlike embrace. The sour stale odours of his body filled her nostrils.

'I'm sorry, Sally, but it's your own fault. Don't make me hurt you! Don't make me! Don't!'

His voice was catching in his throat, his chest heaved with dry sobs. He crushed her to him, squeezing the breath from her, making her gag on the smell of his sweat. Suddenly he froze.

'Listen!' he hissed.

She had heard it too, a distant but loud crashing sound, a shearing of metal mingled with the thump of a heavy impact. The jarring violent sounds hung in the air for long seconds. The man had turned his head towards the sound and she caught a glimpse of him in full profile. For the first time she saw the glint of his real eye behind the sunglasses, an animal not a plastic sheen. She accounted it almost a victory, like finding a chink in his armour.

He rose and took a step towards the door, then hesitated. His body seemed to be pulling him one way and then the other, towards the cause of the sound outside, then back to Sally. He must have come to a decision. He darted into the kitchen then re-emerged a moment later carrying a tea towel. Before she realized what was happening he had twisted and wrapped it round her mouth, tying it at the base of her skull. He headed for the door.

'Ssh!' he said, redundantly in the circumstances, turning back to look at her and putting a finger to his lips.

He started to go then paused again. He snapped his fingers, as if suddenly recollecting something. What might have been a smile creased the corners of his mouth. He reached for the cassette recorder on the table and pressed the play switch. Then, with almost a guilty air, as if he'd committed a schoolboy indiscretion, he grabbed at the door handle and bolted outside.

Sally choked on the gag. The taste of the cloth on her tongue made her nauseous, but it had been tied on hastily, not well, and she forced herself to tear and chew at it with her teeth. In a few moments she had succeeded in working it almost free of her upper lip. She couldn't have managed much of a scream, but at least she could breathe. Her chest was heaving, her body and mind were dizzy with panic. She screwed up her face in concentration, tried to regulate her breathing, get some oxygen into her lungs. She was on the verge of tears. She fought an intense internal battle for control of herself, and eventually she won.

Anger fuelled her. A dark wordless suspicion had been nudging at the back of her consciousness ever since she'd realized that she wasn't a random victim, but seeing that mutilated photograph had given it substance. She may not have known the man's name, she didn't care, but she knew who he was. It was *him*: the burglar; the anonymous caller; the plague of her life – the bastard . . . she knew it absolutely, without any doubt. He had followed her down here, stalked her, planned this whole thing as part of some sick fantasy. It hadn't been Dick he'd been after last Sunday, it had been her. Poor Dick had simply got in his way, as had Jason. She shuddered at the thought of what he might have done had Lizzie disturbed him during the break-in; what he might have done to her. Well, he would do it now, wouldn't he? She blanked out the thought. She wasn't going to play the victim. Helpless as she was, she would fight him with every last drop of her strength and will.

She heard a voice. She supposed for a moment that it was the television, then she remembered that the volume was off. It was coming from the cassette recorder on the table. It was his voice, tinny and distorted through the tiny speaker. The speech was indistinct, mumbled and slurred, it took her a while to adjust her ears to it. There was a slight accent she hadn't noticed before, a hint of an original country burr.

'Don't be upset by the blood, Sally, don't . . . I don't want you to have to look at these things, but I've got to protect you, look after you. You mustn't trust these bad men. Don't trust anyone but me. They don't want me around, they want to keep you for themselves, I know

185

the way they think, but I'll find you, don't worry . . .
soon . . .'

The voice droned on, flatly inexpressive in tone but
charged with an intense undercurrent of suppressed emo-
tion. It was rambling, maudlin and incoherent. He stopped
and started constantly, the quality of the acoustic changing
every time, as if he had been carrying the recorder with
him about the house and making fresh mutterings as and
when the mood took him. The audio tape, like the video
tapes, must have been made over a period of time. She
saw that the TV in the corner was showing one of her
commercials. She had appeared in three during her career,
as a housewife agonizing over her choice of washing
powder, as a young mum experimenting with a new brand
of nappy, and as a busy high-powered executive demon-
strating the importance of wearing ladder-free tights. This
was the housewife. No one could say that her career had
lacked excitement and variety.

'Oh Sally, I know that you'll be here with me one day
soon, I know it. I've always loved you, ever since the first
time I saw you on TV. That wasn't the *Eastenders*, I only
found out you'd been in that later, I had to get the tape
through a fan club – it cost me a bit, I'll tell you. No, the
first time I saw you was when you were in that episode
of *Frost*, you know, the one where you played the doctor's
wife. I thought you were the most beautiful woman I'd
ever seen, then I saw you in the ads. I think about you
all the time. I can't go on without you, I want you at my
side, where you belong. Why aren't you here?'

His voice had risen in pitch. It subsided again, lapsed
into a self-pitying whine. And so it went on, and on. The
monologues were shapeless and unconnected. It all would
have sounded banal had it not been so chilling. The man
was obsessed. Surely he wouldn't harm her, then, not if
she was the object of his adoration? It was not a thought
she could cling to with any conviction. It was her image

the man was obsessed with, not her. He had already used her roughly, notwithstanding his cack-handed apologies. Having to listen to his interminable onanistic fantasies did little to soothe her fears.

'I dream of you night after night. When I wake up you are the first thing I think of. Always. When I sit down at the table to eat I close my eyes and when I open them again I see you sitting opposite me. We're having a candlelit meal, all romantic like. I tell you how beautiful you are, and you smile at me shyly. You are looking stunning, in your black dress, with your hair done up, just like that picture in *You* magazine. At the end of the meal I sweep you up in my arms and carry you upstairs. You gaze at me adoringly. I take off your dress, and lay you out on the bed, and feast my eyes on you. I desire you, and I know you want me too, you're begging for it. I take down your panties . . .'

'Dream on, you sick weirdo!' Sally mumbled through her gag.

Her voice, though muffled, was firm and unwavering. She was still scared, of course, but contempt had dulled the worst of her fear. If he was going to do anything to her he would have to untie her first, and she would fight him all the way. Even if he held his knife to her throat she would fight him. And if she once got hold of that knife she'd stick it in him. She'd never in her life even hit anyone, but she'd stab this man to death without compunction. She flexed her bound arms and legs, tried to prepare herself physically and mentally for the struggle ahead. She blocked out the inane witterings coming from the recorder. She closed her eyes, imagined the opportunities that would be presented the moment he untied her, considered how best she could use them. She wouldn't trip and fall if she could get away from him a second time. She'd head for the house she'd seen through the trees and she would get there first. He had tried to prevent her from screaming, that must mean there were people in the vicinity. Why else would he have gagged her?

The front door opened and the man walked in, glancing behind him as he did so. He went directly to the windows and checked that the curtains were properly closed. He didn't look at Sally. Instead he went through to the hall. When he came back in he was brandishing his knife, a wicked heavy black-handled instrument with a curving tip and an inch of serrated edge on the blade. He stuck the weapon into his belt.

'Been a car smash,' he said, though whether he was addressing Sally she couldn't tell. He was back at one of the windows again, peering through the slit in the curtains. 'No ambulance yet.'

Yet . . . Sally sensed her pulse quicken. There would be sirens soon, people nearby, maybe the police. The man looked agitated. If only he would untie her she would have a chance.

After a minute he turned away from the window and came and stood in front of her. He turned off the cassette machine and stared at her in silence. She didn't stare back. It was pointless trying to meet his eyes when she couldn't see them. She kept her focus on the knife in his belt. More minutes passed.

'I've dreamt of this moment for so long,' he said, his voice tinged with awe. 'I didn't know it was going to be today, though. I didn't plan that you should come here, but when I saw you with that scumbag in the car park I knew it couldn't go on, I couldn't let these other men pester you any more. Why do you do it, Sally, are you trying to wind me up? You flaunt yourself. I hated you last night – do you know that? – When I saw you go into the house with that Philip man, that . . . that . . . Why do you make me hate you, Sally? I love you, why do you treat me like shit?'

His voice had risen to a tremulous whine, by now a

familiar sound. Sally didn't react. She kept staring ahead.

'Well, let's not talk about that now,' he said after a long pause, sounding calmer. 'You're here, that's the important thing. If I'd known you were coming I'd have made the place nicer, but I didn't know, did I? I'm going to go upstairs now, make it nice for you. You'll be grateful. You wait and see.'

He reached out a hand towards her. She refused to flinch. She stayed stock-still as he stroked her hair, even as she inwardly recoiled. His hand travelled tentatively down her face. His middle finger traced a line from her chin to her breastbone. Slowly, clumsily, he undid the top button of her T-shirt. He hesitated. She heard him swallow, she sensed both excitement and uncertainty. She didn't even blink. His hand fell back to his side.

'You be patient, all right?' he murmured through dry lips. He turned away from her suddenly and went through the green curtains.

She heard his footsteps on the stairs and in the room above. She heard drawers and cupboard doors being slammed. The floorboards protested, he seemed to be moving heavy furniture about. After a while the sounds stopped. She had no idea how long he was gone, but it must have been at least twenty minutes. When he reappeared he was wearing a clean dark blue shirt and had combed and gelled his hair. He came and stood in front of her again and she smelt his toothpaste and his aftershave. He must have thought he looked the business.

'Remember this?' he said, holding up her black Versace dress in his hands.

She didn't answer. No doubt he had her missing nightdress upstairs too.

'It was what you were wearing the first time I saw you, remember?'

She had to look up at his face. She was puzzled. What was he talking about?

'The first time, you remember? Your flatmate answered the door, she wanted to take the flowers, but I said it was your name on the card, you had to sign. I'd insisted on doing the job, you see. I was in the florist's when the order came, I heard the girl repeat your name and address. I couldn't believe it, I really couldn't. I had to see with my own eyes if it was really you. And it was. You were sitting on the sofa, in this dress, talking on the phone. I was jealous at first, but then I realized you were only talking to your mother. You smiled at me when you saw the flowers. I could hardly hold the pad straight as you were signing your name. You smiled again when you'd finished. At me, Sally. It was fate that brought us together.'

His voice was trembling. He might almost have been crying. She stared at him blankly, but out of amazement, not ignorance. She was beginning to understand now. He was volatile and unpredictable and without doubt danger-ous, but she could manipulate him, if she dared. She had to dare, there was no choice.

She made a noise through the gag, exaggerating its con-straining effect. He came behind her and untied it. She enjoyed the sensation of opening her mouth wide again and taking in air.

'I'd like to put on the dress,' she said in a calm steady voice. That was all. It was on the tip of her tongue to ask him to untie her, to tell him that she couldn't get into the dress unless he released her first, but she didn't say it. Her motive would appear transparent. She had to leave it to him to make the logical deduction.

He stared at her long and hard. She felt him gauging her, trying to probe the intent behind her eyes. She kept them blank. She wasn't going to betray herself now with a careless flicker of excitement; she was much too good an actress for that.

He put the dress down on the table and knelt in front of her. He took the knife from his belt and cut away the ropes round her ankles. Then he walked to the back of the chair and freed her hands. He put away the knife once more and indicated for her to take the dress. He stepped back, crossed his arms, and stood watching her intently. Clearly he expected her to strip in front of him.

'I have to use the bathroom,' she announced firmly.

Her request evidently took him by surprise. He looked disgruntled. With a little shake of the head he indicated the green velvet curtain, saying in a gruff voice:

'Through there. Hurry up.'

She picked up the dress and went through the curtain. The staircase was ahead of her, the bathroom to the left. There were no other rooms on this floor. She went in and closed the door after her.

There was no lock, nor anything that could have been wedged under the handle. Had there been it could only have offered her temporary respite anyway, for the door had a frosted glass panel and wouldn't have kept him out for more than a few seconds. There was no avenue of escape, of course, but she'd known there wouldn't be, otherwise he wouldn't have let her out of his sight. The window was tiny, high up in the wall and again of frosted glass.

It was a small cramped room, smelling of mildew. There was no bath, just a toilet and a shower unit with a plastic curtain. She put down the toilet seat, stood on it and tried to see out of the window. It was locked and didn't look like it had been opened in years. Her legs felt weak and her ankles were very sore. She rubbed her calves to try and restore the circulation. She'd thought about bolting for the door as soon as the last rope had come off, but she'd realized in time that she would be unsteady on her feet and would have little chance of making it. She would need a few minutes yet to recover the strength in her legs. She hadn't been able to see her watch before, but looking at the time now she guessed that she had been tied to the chair for nearly an hour. With a sense of shock she realized that the play had already started. She hoped that her understudy knew her lines.

A shadow fell across the frosted glass door. She reached behind her and flushed the toilet.

'Hurry up,' he said through the door, his voice a mixture of impatience and suspicion.

'I have to get cleaned up,' she answered.

She turned on the sink taps and let them run noisily. After a bit the shadow moved away from the door.

She looked around urgently, trying to find anything that could help her. There was a small medicine cabinet in the wall, but it was empty. It didn't take her long to do an inventory of the entire bathroom. There was a ragged handtowel, a tiny sliver of soap and a bottle of household disinfectant.

She unscrewed the lid of the bottle and peered inside. It was powerful, concentrated stuff. She took it to the shower, flicked it at the plastic curtain. The liquid squirted out freely, marking the slimy material with thick green pungent patches. If she could only get her aim right, and get it into his eyes, it would disable him for precious seconds.

She took off her jeans and T-shirt and put on the black dress. It was tighter, and shorter, than she remembered; hardly designed for sprinting in. She strapped her sandals back on and made sure they were buckled tight. Carefully she rolled up her jeans and T-shirt and inserted the bottle of disinfectant through the middle. The lidless spout was just sticking out. She covered it lightly with the sleeve of her shirt.

'Come on!' he said anxiously, his shadow appearing on the glass once more. 'Hurry up!'

Instinctively Sally checked her face in the mirror. She looked pale and drawn and by no means at her best. But she was no longer a woman of mere flesh and blood. She

192

was a totem, a fantasy and fetish incarnate. If she was not dressed to kill she was at least dressed to maim.

'I'm coming,' she said.

She closed her eyes and prayed. Then she opened the door and stepped out into the hall.

14

There was an odd discoloured damp patch in the ceiling. It was next to the light fitting, a tarnished brass hook from which a plain paper Chinese lampshade depended. The patch was grey, fringed with black, like a storm-cloud hovering amidst the white cumulus of plaster. Backed like a weasel. Very like a whale.

He wondered how long he had been staring at the ceiling. Consciousness was taking such a long time to return. Was he dreaming? As soon as he thought to ask himself the question he knew that he wasn't. He wished more than anything that he had been. If he had been asleep he wouldn't have felt his aching head.

It ached rhythmically, in time with his sluggish pulse. Pain, pause, pain, pause, went the maddening insistent beat. That patch on the ceiling was annoying him. Very like a whale. What was that? It was a play, wasn't it? Was it a part he'd played? He didn't think so. He did play parts, though, that was his job. Shouldn't he have been doing it now? What was the time?

He lifted his wrist. He couldn't see his watch. Why was he wearing that silly frilly cuff? No wonder he couldn't see his watch. He knew it was under there somewhere, he could hear it ticking. It was such a loud, annoying sound, it set his teeth on edge. But it wasn't coming from his wrist. He turned his head slowly to the side, feeling his cheek sink slowly into the soft comfortable pillow.

There was a big old-fashioned alarm clock on the bedside table. He stared at it, and after a supreme effort of concentration the face slid into focus. It had just gone eight o'clock.

It hit him like an electric bolt. He was off, he'd missed his entrance! His brain and body twitched together, he leapt up off the bed. Immediately his head dissolved with giddiness and the strength drained from his legs. He sagged and crumpled.

He had fallen on to bare wood. His ear, pressed tight to a floorboard, began to pick up distant vibrations. Then he heard distinct footsteps. Someone was coming.

The door was thrown open and a huge pair of feet tramped in. He had never seen such monstrous Doc Martens. Was he in the lair of an elephantine skinhead?

Hands seized him under the arms and lifted him effortlessly. No, it wasn't a skinhead at all, but a giant with sandy hair and freckles. The giant dropped him back on to the bed, straightened out his legs, then stepped back and stared at him, shaking his head slowly from side to side.

'I don't believe it,' said the giant in a piping girlish voice. 'I just don't believe it.'

The giant's face hovered over the end of the bed, like a Halloween pumpkin on a stick. Why was this big stupid face gawping at him? Why was it putting on such a silly voice? With enormous effort he succeeded in raising himself up on his elbows.

'Do you know who I am?' he demanded in his most pompous stentorian voice.

'Yes,' said the giant in a hushed tone. 'You're Philip Fletcher.'

'Oh. Am I?'

Philip fell back on to the pillow. He was staring again at that blasted ceiling. The damp patch didn't look like a weasel or a whale or anything at all. It looked like a bloody damp patch.

'I don't believe it,' he heard the giant saying again. 'I just don't believe it . . .'

The giant tut-tutted mysteriously to himself and went out of the room. He banged the door shut so hard that the bedstead shook. His thin tremulous voice squeaked from the other side:

'Sorry!'

His footsteps receded. A sort of silence settled, marred only by the heavy ticking of the clock.

Philip lay on the bed staring at the damp patch in the ceiling, trying to coerce some kind of order from the disordered pulp that passed for his brain. A baffling kaleidoscope of images jostled for attention behind his eyes. His headache was getting worse, it was impossible to concentrate. Had he really driven into a tree? The image was potent, he didn't see how he could have imagined it, but he didn't drive, he didn't even have a car, so how could he have hit a tree? Was he fantasizing, or suffering from amnesia? What was he doing here? Who was the ginger giant? What was going on?

'Sally!'

He sat up suddenly. That's why he was here, because of Sally. They'd kidnapped her, they were holding her against her will. He'd come straight from the theatre, that was why he was wearing the frilly shirt, these silly clothes. They'd taken his shoes. He stared with horror at his stockinged feet. What play was he meant to be in? That didn't matter. Why had they taken his shoes? To stop him running away, of course.

Waves of blackness rolled over him. His eyes wouldn't stop blurring, he was tottering on the edge of consciousness. He bit his lip, hard. He couldn't pass out now, he had to stay awake. Sally was in terrible danger, and so was he. They were both prisoners. How many were in the gang? At least three: Olive, the ginger giant, and the dark man. The dark man had a knife, he'd taken Sally in the van which had almost killed him by the bridge. They were a ruthless gang, a trio of scheming fiendish criminals. He had to escape from their clutches, save Sally . . .

He tried to focus again on the clock, to work out how long he had been lying there. What if the clock was slow, or fast? What did it matter? He shook his head angrily. He was wasting time on insignificant details. In any case, there was a telephone on the table, he could always phone up the speaking clock and confirm the exact time. What he had to be doing now was figuring out some way to escape. If he could find his shoes it would be a . . .

He stared dumbly at the telephone. It had to be disconnected. No, he could see the lead going into the wall. It had to be broken then. He picked up the receiver and slowly, disbelievingly, put it to his ear. He listened in mute amazement to the dialling tone. The criminal fiends had made a fatal mistake!

He jabbed out 999. He held his breath, it seemed to be taking an age to get a connection. Then it began to ring – and ring, and ring, and ring. He was going frantic. At last the ringing stopped. He heard a woman asking whether he wanted fire, police or –

'Police!' he yelped. 'Police! Police! Police!'

'Philip!' called Olive's voice from the other side of the door. 'Can I come in?'

Philip froze.

'Hello?' said a man on the telephone.

The door swung open, revealing Olive, who was holding a tray, and, standing behind her, the ginger giant, who was holding a shotgun.

'I'd like a four seasons pizza with extra pepperoni topping,' Philip said quickly into the phone, and slammed it down.

'Now you know there's no reason to send out for anything,' said Olive reprovingly. 'You know there's always a good square meal for you at Heron Farm. Isn't that right, Sean?'

'That's right, Mum,' said the ginger giant, nodding as he shouldered his shotgun.

'Don't shoot!' gasped Philip, flopping back weakly on to the pillow.

Sean looked at Philip blankly. Olive chortled. She brought the tray round to the side of the bed.

'You are a one, Philip,' she said, clearing the clock away from the table and making enough space to slide in the tray. 'Always ready with a quip, eh? Didn't I tell you, Sean.'

'Yes, Mum.'

'Now you run along, all right?'

'Shall I bring the camera later, Mum, like you said?'

'Yes, but leave us for now, will you. Philip and I have got a lot to talk about.'

'Yes, Mum. Oh, and er . . .' His voice dropped to an embarrassed whisper. 'Will you explain about the motor?'

'Of course I will. Don't worry, he'll understand.'

The giant looked relieved. He gave the barrel of his shotgun a tap as he went out.

'Hope he likes rabbit stew.'

Olive laughed indulgently at her son.

'Always thinking of his stomach that boy. Same as you, Philip, eh? Well, don't worry, I'll see you're properly taken care of.'

She flashed a huge grin at him. Her eyes flickered manically. A foot-long knife glinted in her hand.

'Please!' whispered Philip almost noiselessly. He'd lost what little motive power he'd had a minute ago, he hadn't even strength to lift a finger to protect himself. It was like that film, *Misery*. Olive was playing the Kathy Bates part, she was going to cut his legs off, keep him crippled and her prisoner, and no one would ever know –

'There! I hope that's big enough for you.'

He blinked at her. The knife had gone. She was offering him a piece of chocolate cake on a plate.

'Fresh out the oven,' she said proudly. 'It'll crumble in your mouth. You know, I'm sorry if this sounds stupid, but my head's been so full today I keep forgetting things, everyday things I know I know – if you see what I mean! Now, tell me, and forgive me for asking, but – it is one sugar, isn't it?'

She had put down the plate on the bed and was holding a cup of tea in one hand and a pair of tongs with a sugar lump in the other. She cocked her head expectantly.

'Well?'

'Why are you doing this?' asked Philip grimly.

'Now that is a silly question, isn't it? You know there's nothing I wouldn't do for you.'

'Nothing?' he snapped back.

'Nothing at all,' she answered evenly.

'Then release me.'

'I'm sorry?'

'Please release me, let me go.'

He frowned. Where had he heard that line before?

'You know I can't do that, Philip.'

'You must release me.'

'I can't.'

'You must, I have to be free, it's a matter of life and death!'

'Oh, Philip!'

Olive turned away dramatically, spilling tea on to the floor. She put the cup down, mopped her hand with a tissue and then her eyes. She wandered listlessly to the window and stared out wearing a tragic expression.

'Oh, Philip, I can't believe you'd be so cruel. After all the years I've waited patiently. I always knew you'd come, I never stopped hoping. Sean didn't believe me, he thought I was a bit nutty or something; he denies it but

I know what he tells his friends. But he knew today all right. He was so upset, I can't begin to tell you, about smashing up your nice car, you getting hurt and all. It wasn't his fault, though, he swears and I believe him. You have such a lot on your mind, you get careless sometimes, and Sean's such a good safe driver I know it wasn't him. I hope that doesn't sound disloyal. He'd do anything to make it up to you. He wanted to drive you to hospital, but I wouldn't let him. I'll nurse him, I said, it's what he'd expect, it's what he'd want, and there's nothing broken. I've put your wig in a safe place, by the way. I hope you didn't mind me taking it off, but I couldn't bandage your head with it on, and I had to do that, even though it was only a little cut, a graze really. It was so sweet of you to come and see me in your romantic costume, you looked like Errol Flynn. Oh Philip . . . I really did think you would want it this way, I only ever want to do what's best for you, but now you start saying these . . . things to me and, and it's very hard to take, that's all.'

She was still looking out of the window. She didn't see his arm stretching stealthily across the bedspread. By the time she turned back to him it was too late.

He snatched the knife from the tray and sprang to his feet. His legs began to buckle but he forced himself to stay upright by sheer act of will. He gritted his teeth and clasped the knife belligerently in both hands.

'What have you done with Sally?'

'Beg pardon?'

'Don't play dumb with me, Olive. Where's Sally?'

Olive's eyes were wide with concern. Momentarily she seemed lost for words.

'Sally who?' she managed at last.

Philip swayed. He could hardly keep his balance, he felt disoriented and nauseous. He didn't understand what was going on. It was all so confusing and his head hurt to buggery.

'Sally. I know you've got her. I saw the van parked here, you see, the other night. I know it's the same one.'

'Philip, are you all right?'

'Don't try and mess with me, Olive. I'm armed!'

'Perhaps Sean was right, I should have called the ambulance. Maybe you've got a bit of concussion.'

'Concussion'll be the least of your worries if you don't answer my questions. I've got your knife. Ha!'

He waved it into the space between them. She didn't react.

'That's a cake knife, Philip. I think you'd better sit down, don't you?'

He was reluctant to agree with her, but it was a very good idea. He grabbed the headboard and lowered himself down on to the edge of the bed. He groaned.

'Oh God . . .'

'All right, Philip, now suppose you tell me what's going on. I can't make head nor tail of it. Who is this Sally girl?'

'My co-star, Sally Blair.'

'Never heard of her.'

'She's here, Olive, I know it.'

'Not in this house she isn't.'

'Oh yeah? Then how do you explain the van?'

'What's this van you keep on about?'

'The white van that's parked out front.'

'Oh, that van –'

'So you don't deny it! Sally went off in the white van. That's how I know she's in this house.'

'Why would she be in this house? That's Jeffrey's van.'

'Huh?'

She'd just said she couldn't make head nor tail of it. He was none too clear himself.

'Jeffrey? Who's Jeffrey? Is that your accomplice?'

'What would I want with an accomplice? No, Philip, Jeffrey's my tenant, he rents a cottage off us, just over there.'

She was pointing out of the window. She sounded very matter-of-fact, not like an arch-criminal mastermind at all. Cogs were turning ever so slowly in the back of his brain.

'You mean . . .'

You mean I'm a complete bloody fool? he asked himself. He remembered walking past the cottage by the rape field and looking in through the windows. He rested an elbow on one knee and put his head in his hand.

'This Jeffrey, Olive, he's nothing to do with you, right? You're not working together?'

'No of course we don't work together. We're farmers, he delivers things.'

'Oh God . . . Olive, I need my shoes.'

'I don't think you should get up, Philip, you need to –'

'I've got to, Olive, it's life and death, I told you. Life and death.'

'Well, in that case you'd better put them on. They're on the floor next to you.'

To his bemusement he saw that they were. She bent down and helped him put them on.

'Your coat's hanging up in the –'

'I don't need it, Olive, I just need your help.'

'Of course, I'll do anything, you know that.'

'Yes, I think I do. Give me a hand, will you?'

She helped him to his feet. He rested his hands on her shoulders and stared down into her big blue childlike eyes. He knew as he looked at her that she was incapable of deceiving anyone, except possibly herself. He was beginning to understand a lot of things now. The fog in his brain was lifting.

'Olive, listen carefully, please, we don't have much time. There's something I've got to tell you about Jeffrey . . .'

202

15

She had been half expecting him to be in the hallway, but he was in the living room. He was watching her, though. He had pulled the green curtain to one side so as to have an unrestricted view of the bathroom door. His neck was hunched into his shoulders; his arms hung tensely at an angle from his body, ending in closed fists.

He was standing in front of the television, midway between the front door and the kitchen, the two avenues of escape. He had moved the sofa away from the wall and into the middle of the room so that it faced him. The room was less gloomy than before; he had turned on the main light. She noticed that the TV image was static. He must have pressed the pause button.

'That's wrong,' he said.

His lips barely moved; she could only just hear him. She stopped, just inside the room.

She stared at where his eyes should be. She had to get him to remove his sunglasses. She felt herself begin to tremble. She had been strong in the bathroom, strong and determined. Now that she was facing him her plan didn't seem so clever. She had to make him uncover his eyes.

'Wrong,' he said again, this time barely even sounding the word, merely mouthing it.

'What's –'

'Be quiet!'

He sounded peevish, like a thwarted child; he even stamped his foot. Sally stood very still.

'Your hair's wrong. Should be up. Like in the picture.'

'But –'

'Don't talk!'

He stamped his foot harder. His thick neck muscles were taut and corrugated; a lumpy vein stood out on his broad pale forehead. He seemed to be fighting to control himself, and losing. He stabbed the air with a stubby finger.

'Sit there!'

Before she had been able to make some kind of contact, however rudimentary, but now he wouldn't even let her speak. His peevishness was entirely in character. He *was* a child, a stupid, selfish, immature reasonless baby in an oversized body. Had he not been so dangerous he would have been pathetic.

'I said sit. There!'

He was pointing at the sofa. Though it stuck in the craw she had to obey him. If she tried for the door now he'd have plenty of time to intercept her, and he would be on his guard. She had to let him get closer, then take him by surprise. She sat down carefully on the sofa, putting her clothes bundle in the gap between her and the arm. She kept hold of the bottle with her right hand; with her left she smoothed down her dress.

'You look like a tart,' he said bitterly.

She didn't look up, but sat exactly as before, her eyes at the level of his belt, and his knife. She didn't want to antagonize him, and nor did she want him to see how frightened she was. She felt more vulnerable now than she had when tied to the chair.

He walked to the back of the sofa. She heard him pacing up and down, but she didn't dare look round. He must have had the remote control in his hand, because the VCR gave a sudden click and the tape began to play again. She saw his ghost reflected dimly in the television screen; he was hovering behind her left shoulder.

'You tart!' he said, almost swallowing the word in his anger.

On the tape was another episode of *Paramedics*. It showed her in bed with an actor called Glenn, one of her regular co-stars. It had been a plot development that hadn't gone anywhere, a feeble attempt to inject some love interest into the sagging storyline. She and Glenn were lying next to each other with the sheet pulled up to their chins, kissing tonguelessly. That was all. When they had stopped kissing they lay together chastely and exchanged lines of excruciatingly wooden dialogue. It was a peak-time show, there was no nudity, and certainly no sex.

'How can you do that, with another man? I know he's touching you under the sheets, I know what he's doing with his hands, why do you let him, why don't you make him keep his filthy hands to himself?'

She had no idea what Glenn had done with his hands, but they hadn't been anywhere near her. Glenn was gay. She remembered that during the interminable breaks between takes he had kept her graphically informed of precisely what he had got up to with a dentist called Eamonn the previous night. It had been quite an education, for Eamonn as much as for her she suspected.

'I know why you let them touch you. You like it, don't you? It's disgusting. You shouldn't do it. Don't you understand how it hurts me, you being a slut? Are you trying to wind me up, or what? To make me jealous, is that it? I hate it, you being a slut. I won't have it, you hear?'

He was pacing heavily. His breathing was fast and shallow. The strain in his voice was acute.

'No more, you understand? No more. Flaunting yourself in your short skirts. It's got to stop. Showing everyone your legs. It's immoral. Don't you have any respect for me? I've warned you, you wouldn't listen. I'll stop it, I will. If I hadn't put that bastard in hospital the other night you'd have let him have you, wouldn't you? Like that Philip. Don't think I don't know what you two got up to. I followed you to his place, I saw you go in with him. How many times did you do it then? You cheated on me. I'll kill him if I ever see him again, I'll slice him, I'll stitch him, you'll see. I won't have you whoring. No more.'

She saw him move in the reflection of the TV, but she didn't have time to get away. One hand seized her by the hair and yanked her head back, the other grabbed her by the throat. She clawed with all her strength at his fingers but his grip was immovable. One thick hand was all he needed to crush her windpipe. She stared with helpless bulging eyes into his mad upside-down hate-filled face.

The pressure on her throat was excruciating. She couldn't breathe. She dug into him with her nails, but he didn't react, his grip was iron, inflexible. She felt consciousness begin to slip away. His face was inches from hers, a screwed-up livid mask. She stared into the blank dark lenses of his glasses. Something stirred in her fading memory.

She let go of him and thrust her right hand into the folded bundle of her clothes. With the other she grabbed at his sunglasses. She caught the frame with her nails and flicked them off. He jerked his head away, instinctively loosening his hold on her hair and throat. She looked for the first time into his brown unremarkable eyes. They were wide like a startled animal's. He was almost comical in his grotesque surprise.

He let go of her hair and joined both hands together round her throat. She kept her eyes on his, and took her mark. As his face dipped in again towards her she snapped up her arm and jerked the disinfectant bottle at his face.

A spurt of thick green liquid splashed off the bridge of

his nose. He gasped. Too late he threw his palms protectively across his face. He screamed.

He reeled away in agony, howling and tearing at his eyes. Sally rolled off the sofa, choking, and staggered to her feet. She was weak with shock, she tottered like a drunk. The man's delirious yells acted like a spur. She ran to the front door.

It was locked. How could it be locked, was there a catch? Frantically she felt all round with her fingers. There wasn't. He must have double-locked it with a key.

A ripping noise made her turn. He had fallen into the green curtain and torn it from its rail. He was on his knees, lashing out in her direction with his fists, screaming incoherent abuse. Though his eyes must have been burning he could see enough to know where she was. She bolted for the kitchen and he came scuttling across the floor towards her.

The kitchen door was locked. She yanked at the handle, again and again, numb with disbelief. He had locked both doors. She could see the trees and open fields through the glass door but she couldn't get out. Her mind was blank. She couldn't think what to do. The man was in the kitchen.

She tried to get out of his way, but there was nowhere to go. He hit out and caught her in the face. She fell stunned to the linoleum floor and he crashed down on top of her, knocking the breath from her lungs. Before she could gasp in any more his knee was in her spine and his hands were round her throat.

Spots danced before her eyes. She was hallucinating, her brain squeezing out one last bizarre image before death. An apparition had materialized in the glass of the door, a half-familiar man in theatrical costume with a bandage round his head. She could have almost sworn she heard him banging to get in.

There was an almighty crashing sound and suddenly

the air was full of flying glass. She saw it falling in thick irregular shards across the floor, she felt a sudden stab and watched a fresh bright smear of blood appear on her arm. This was no hallucination. The pressure on her back and throat had ceased, the man was climbing off her.

'Unhand her, you rogue!' demanded Philip Fletcher in his most magnificently foppish tone.

He didn't look too steady on his feet, which considering he'd just walked through a glass door perhaps wasn't so surprising. His eyes were glazed and oddly expressionless. He seemed to be having trouble remembering which part he was playing.

'Now be a sensible chap and give me the knife,' he said in the manner of Jack Warner in *The Blue Lamp*. 'Don't be silly now, Jeffrey.'

Jeffrey? Sally looked up at him out of the corner of her eye. Deprived of his anonymity he would have seemed a mundane sort of monster now had it not been for the knife in his hand.

'Philip! Watch out!'

It ought to have been an unnecessary warning, but he was so sluggish he barely seemed to move as the blade came flashing towards him. The monster Jeffrey swung his free forearm under Philip's chin and pinned him back against the doorframe. The point of the knife hovered an inch from his face.

'I told you to keep away from her!' Jeffrey screamed, his voice hideously distorted with pain and rage. 'I told you!'

Sally seized a misshapen triangle of broken glass and plunged the jagged point into his calf. Philip had just sufficient wits left to shove him away.

Jeffrey staggered back towards the living room, clutching at the wound in his leg. With an anguished howl he pulled the glass shard out.

'Run!' shouted Sally. 'For God's sake, Philip, run!'

She was on her feet and pushing him away. But there was nowhere for them to go. A quivering mountain of flesh blocked the door.

'Out of the way, love,' said the fattest woman in Sussex as she somehow squeezed her way into the tiny kitchen, flattening them both against the wall.

Sally was stunned. Philip didn't look as if he was all there either. Jeffrey was the first to react. He raised his knife and came hobbling towards them.

The fat woman levelled a shotgun at his chest and fired both barrels at point-blank range.

Sally was sitting on the floor covered in blood and broken glass. She was disoriented, half frozen with shock and half deaf with the noise of the shot. Philip looked much the same. The fat woman knelt down, dropped the gun and cradled his head in her arms. There was something oddly familiar about her. The woman noticed Sally staring at her and gave her a reassuring smile.

'Because I love him,' she said simply.

16

Everyone at the theatre had thought the media attention after the attack on Dick Jones excessive. It was like a gentle breeze in comparison with the hurricane that broke following the revelations made in what shortly became known worldwide as the Maniac Stalker case.

The theatre and its environs were clogged with newshounds sniffing for scents. Journalists with pads and microphones, with photographers and camera crews in tow, ran around arbitrarily sucking up interviews like out-of-control vacuum cleaners. The theatre, the car park, Heron Farm, the cottage, all the locations of the drama soon became as well known to the viewing nation as Ramsey Street or Albert Square. The newspapers fought tooth and nail with chequebooks drawn to nab exclusives. Rumour had it that Olive Vibash had signed with Max Clifford, that Tom Cruise and Nicole Kidman were going to play Philip Fletcher and Sally Blair in a Hollywood film. The world gasped and was amazed. Except, that is, for Philip Fletcher, who wondered what was wrong with Philip Fletcher playing Philip Fletcher.

Certainly he was in demand if the theatre box office was anything to go by. Ticket sales for *The Country Wife* had been frankly disappointing, and would scarcely have been encouraged by some decidedly modest notices. But from the morning that the story broke the phones didn't stop ringing. Within forty-eight hours every ticket for the entire run had been sold and the talk was on again of a West End transfer. The maddening thing for Philip was that he was *hors de combat* and unable initially to bask in the acclaim.

The doctors were unanimous in refusing him leave from bed. He had been badly concussed, he needed rest and wasn't to be allowed to venture out of sight until the results of tests and scans had been fully analysed. In all he was kept in his pyjamas for a whole week. It was the most frustrating period of his life.

Sally missed just two performances. She had been badly shaken, but had suffered only minor cuts and bruises. The doctors wanted her to take it easy, but they had no medical reason to keep her in hospital and were powerless to prevent her from leaving. Work, she told them, was the only therapy she needed. She said the same to the journalists who descended on her in swarms, but declined to give any in-depth interviews, despite the massive financial inducements. Two publishers wrote asking her to name her price for a book. She replied that she didn't know how to write a book, but it transpired that that really didn't matter. They just wanted her name on the cover and her photograph on the jacket. Sally had always believed that the theatre was a uniquely peculiar profession. She was bemused to discover that the publishing world was every bit as odd.

Olive was the one prepared to talk, so it was she who got the coverage. There was a national outcry when the story leaked that the Crown Prosecution Service was considering whether or not to bring charges against her. The issue of a hasty denial did nothing to take the wind out of the tabloids' sails, or indeed their sales, and Olive Vibash, dubbed the Annie Oakley of West Sussex, duly became one of the more unlikely heroines of modern times. A keen reader of Sunday exclusives herself, she had no qualms about selling her story. The rumours about media fixers proved unfounded. Instead her son Sean acted as her agent and to everyone's surprise turned out to be remarkably astute. He negotiated a healthy six-figure sum after a competitive auction and followed up with an equally impressive book and serialization deal, having grasped effortlessly in a way that had eluded Sally the mechanics of latter-day literary hire and salary. In this he was no doubt greatly aided by the fact that he had not once actually opened a book himself during the course of his adult life.

Even Jason obtained some healthy financial compensation for his troubles. Shortly after his emergence from intensive care he appeared in a lurid Sunday spread, baring his bandaged chest and pointing to the exact spot in the car park where he had 'stared into the face of death'. Shortly afterwards his new-found celebrity won him a regular role in a daytime television soap, where the absence of any discernible talent was not noticed.

When the papers had tired of the living actors in the drama they turned their attention instead to Jeffrey Forrester. 'He was a bit of a loner', said one of his neighbours, who had clearly read newspaper interviews with the neighbours of homicidal maniacs before. A former class teacher made the equally acute remark that 'he kept himself to himself'. One Sunday publication alone managed to fill four broadsheet pages with observations of this magnitude. The lucky owner of a ten-year-old snapshot of Jeffrey Forrester in the background of a group photo at his local pub cashed in happily.

The police did not succeed in piecing together the full story until much later, by which time media interest had rather faded, though it was by no means spent. He was estranged from his family, had few friends and had never been known to have a regular girlfriend. Not surprisingly it took a while to glean enough character details to be able to paint any kind of a picture. Even then the end result remained hazy.

The police concluded that he had come across Sally purely by chance. Initially they were confused by her testimony, but it seemed that his assertion that he had been in love with her for years could not be borne out by the facts. He was an habitual liar, even to himself. He had had no idea who she was until he'd arrived to deliver Jason's flowers. She had not remembered him because she had not seen him. Liz had signed for the flowers, the docket that confirmed it was found in the firm's files. He must have recognized Sally's face when he glimpsed her through the door. He'd made up other details too. Liz thought it was plausible that she'd been talking to her mother on the phone, but both doubted that she would have changed into the rarely worn Versace for the occasion. His workmates remembered him talking about her endlessly. He had been highly excited. He had told anyone who would listen that he'd seen in the flesh someone famous from the telly.

He had probably obtained Sally's phone number from the firm's records. They denied it, but the relevant files were never under lock and key. Jason had given the number with the address when he'd made the order, in case Sally was out when the delivery arrived. It couldn't be stated absolutely that Jeffrey Forrester had made the phone calls, but the circumstantial evidence made it highly likely.

What no one could explain was the process whereby within the space of a few months the chance encounter with 'a minor celebrity' (Sally's own phrase) had turned into an all-consuming obsession. A variety of pundits, with or without medical qualifications, were invited to comment; others commented without invitation. There was little consensus of opinion. Was he sick or was he evil? Was he an 'organized' offender who had planned every detail of the abduction minutely, or a 'disorganized' one who had made it up as he went along? Had his encounter with Sally set off a freak chain of circumstances, or had she merely acted as a random catalyst on 'an accident waiting to happen'. Her own refusal to speak out only fuelled the debate. After reading endless articles and listening to innumerable talk-shows on the subject few were any the wiser.

Jeffrey Forrester did not have a criminal record. There were no documents, not even a diary. All that survived of him were the rambling monologues on half a dozen cassette tapes, which were never released into the public domain. There were rumours that some other material, allegedly of a photographic nature, had also been found at the cottage, but the authorities never disclosed details. It wasn't much of a legacy for a man who had generated so many column inches. A promised posthumous biography failed to appear for want of material. In the end, ironically, his name was to survive in a legal footnote, when what became known as the Forrester amendment was added to a private members' bill designed to tackle the growing menace of stalking.

Philip's eventual return to the stage, the Monday following his full week of convalescence, was an uninterrupted triumphal progress. Rather than subject himself to repeatedly running the gauntlet, he had requested that the stage be made available for an all-in-one afternoon press conference. Sally declined the invitation to appear with him. With a purely notional show of reluctance Philip prepared to bask in the limelight alone. His casual and unheralded appearance on the stage (carefully modelled on Olivier's first entrance in *Othello*) elicited a smattering of spontaneous applause from the hard-bitten audience.

'Were you scared, Philip?'

'Not as much as on the opening night.'

'How does it feel to be hero of the hour?'

'That sounds a little ephemeral; can't I at least be hero of the week?'

'Is it true that you've been recommended for a gallantry award?'

'I think that should go to Olive Vibash. She was the one who finally saved us.'

'We're a little puzzled by Olive's claim that you two are actually engaged to be married.'

'So am I, to be frank. She's an extraordinary woman, of course, but inclined to exaggeration.'

'Did you know the Maniac Stalker had a knife?'

'Did he know Olive had a shotgun?'

'How did you find his lair?'

'I'd seen the van around, I just put two and two together. Call it instinct, if you like.'

'Intuition?'

'You could call it that if you prefer.'

'Can I quote you on that?'

'You can quote me on anything as long as you spell my name correctly.'

'Have you seen Dick Jones since you got out of hospital?'

'No.'

'Is he still demanding that you be arrested?'

'I don't think so.'

'According to witnesses you had to punch him on the nose before he'd let you have his car keys.'

'Well I can hardly deny what the photographs you've published confirm.'

'Isn't he a bit embarrassed?'

'You'll have to ask him. I'm sure it was a misunderstanding.'

'Who's paying for the damage to his car?'

'Dick has very generously agreed to claim on his

insurance. He says there are no hard feelings and that the matter is closed.'

'I thought you hadn't spoken to him?'

'I'm only repeating what I read in the papers. I can believe what I read in the papers, can't I?'

'Not in his.'

'Gentlemen – and ladies – please! I should tell you that in the theatre it is customary to restrict the eye-gouging to backstage.'

'What are your immediate plans?'

'To finish the run of *The Country Wife* and then perhaps to take a holiday.'

'What about films?'

'I don't have time to visit the cinema just at present.'

'Bet you've had offers.'

'I don't intend to disclose the sordid details of my private life. That's what autobiographies are for.'

'Are you planning to write one?'

'Only if I can think of a suitable subject.'

'Come on, Philip, that sounds a bit modest.'

'I'll try anything once. And now, if you'll excuse me, I'm afraid I have to start preparing for tonight's performance. I have the little matter of a professional engagement to fulfil. If you'd like me to pose for any photographs, I think I can probably spare a couple of minutes . . .'

In the event the photo shoot took around twenty minutes. It still left Philip plenty of time in which to get ready for the show. He had told the stage manager to allow for half an hour.

A handful of photographers was allowed to remain on the strict understanding that they would not take any shots during the actual show. The moment that the curtain came down and the terms of their embargo expired their flashlights exploded into action. The evening had been a monumental success, and the packed house, which had contributed laughter by the bucketload and way beyond the call of duty, rose as one to give the actors a standing ovation. When Sally and Philip came forward together at the end the rest of the cast joined in the applause. Sally looked intensely uncomfortable.

'I hope it isn't like this every night,' she murmured to Philip as they clasped hands and took yet another bow.

'I hope it is.'

For him the whole evening had flashed by in a triumphal blur. He was determined to prolong and savour the last moments. At the very end he descended the stage only with the greatest reluctance. He repaired to his dressing room to accept the plaudits and congratulations of his peers. He was confident that they would shortly be with him because he'd promised free champagne.

They came, they drank him dry, they left again. As they were reducing through natural wastage to a hard core he noticed that Sally was not amongst them. He went along the corridor to her dressing room, knocked and went on in.

'Oh, I'm most terribly sorry . . .'

Sally and the man she had been kissing passionately sprang apart. It took Philip a moment to realize that it was Robert Hammond. All three of them blushed together.

'I'm so sorry,' repeated Philip. 'I shouldn't have barged in.'

'It's all right, Philip,' said Sally hastily.

'I was just going actually,' said Robert, with an entirely unnecessary look at his watch. 'I'll see you over the road then, Sal?'

'Yes. I'll just finish changing.'

She was in a state of marked undress, though how much this was due to changing her costume and how much to Robert was at least questionable.

'Coming over the road for a drink, Philip?' asked Robert.

'Well, I was just coming to see if you were going to have a drink with me.'

'Oh my God!' said Sally.

'The champagne,' said Robert.

'I forgot.'

'So did I.'

'Never mind,' said Philip. 'I can see you were otherwise engaged.'

Sally and Robert exchanged flushed looks. Robert blew her a discreet kiss.

'See you in a minute, then.'

He went out and closed the door. Philip cleared his throat.

'I really must apologize, I shouldn't have –'

'It's quite all right, Philip, please don't say another word.' She laughed and pulled a face. 'It's meant to be a secret, you know.'

'I promise not to tell. I'd better let you finish changing.'

'I'm done now. Please stay a minute. Have a seat.'

She scooped some clothes out of her armchair to make room for him. She perched on the edge of the table.

'All right?' he asked.

'I think so. I take my hat off to you, the way you've handled the press. I'm afraid I couldn't cope with that kind of scrutiny at all.'

'It goes with the territory, I'm afraid. The day of the strolling player is gone with the dinosaurs. We're media commodities these days.'

'What a terrifying thought. The kind of thought that feeds the Jeffrey Forresters of this world.'

'He was a one-off.'

'I hope so, Philip, I hope so . . . You know, it's a funny thing, but I didn't even know what he was called until the end, when you broke through the door and confronted him. It's ridiculous, but as soon as I heard his name I could hardly take him seriously. I had a pet hamster called Jeffrey when I was a kid. Stupid, isn't it?'

'You were extraordinarily brave.'

'I really didn't think he was going to hurt me. He kept saying he loved me, why should he want to kill me?'

'Because he couldn't possess you; he didn't want anyone else to.'

'You've been reading those pop psychiatrists in the papers.'

'Everyone else has a theory. Why can't I?'

'As it happens, I think you're right. One of the articles suggested he was impotent; that may even be right too. He couldn't cope with me as a real woman. I was just a fantasy object, the reality was too terrifying for him. That's why he didn't try to rape me. I don't think he was capable, and his resentment and jealousy made him murderous. Does that sound too pat? All I know for sure is that he would have killed me if you hadn't come along. You were wonderful, Philip, you know I'll never be able to repay you.'

'Please don't, you'll embarrass me. I must say you're looking remarkably well, all things considered.'

'I'm glad you said that. Everyone keeps putting on long faces and lowering their voices when they speak to me; I feel as if I'm in a funeral parlour. It's like they think I'm terribly damaged and fragile and liable to go to pieces at any minute. Perhaps I ought to be like that. Perhaps there's something wrong with me. I'm almost raped and murdered, I see my ex-boyfriend get stabbed in front of me, he almost kills you too, and then he gets blown to pieces in front of my eyes. Hardly a pleasant sight. Why aren't I traumatized? Do you suppose it'll all catch up with me in a little while?'

'Perhaps you're tougher than you think.'

'No. I'm tougher than I *look*, Philip. That's a different matter. I've slept every night since I came out of hospital, slept like a baby. Much better than it's been for months, since this whole thing started. I think it was actually worse when I was getting the phone calls. And after the burglary it was worst of all – not knowing who it was, jumping every time the phone rang, imagining I was being followed. As it happened, I was being followed, but I was a bag of nerves anyway. Now at least I know it's all over and I can get on with my life.'

'And with your career. Don't be too reticent now. I understand why you don't want to rake it all over in public with the press, but at this moment you've got one of the best-known names and faces in the country. Take advantage while you can.'

'Yup. I will. I'd better go over and join Robert, I've got a drink waiting. You coming over?'

'I shouldn't like to cramp his style.'

'Don't, please. I'm sorry you found out about us the way you did, we really were trying to keep it a secret. Please don't spread it round, no one else knows.'

'I shan't say a word to anyone. Goodnight, Sally.'

'Goodnight, darling Philip.'

She flung her arms round him as he rose from his seat and gave him a long clinging hug. When at length he disengaged he retraced his steps down the corridor wistfully with the scent of her hair still filling his nostrils. His dressing room was empty save for Roy Power, who was tipping up empty champagne bottles in search of dregs.

'Fuck off now, Roy, I want to be alone.'

'Really, Philip, I know you've been through a great deal but there's no need –'

Philip grabbed his collar and thrust him out of the door. He dropped into his chair, crossed his feet up on the table and pulled a half-full bottle of Famous Grouse out of the drawer. He tipped away a drop of champagne from the nearest plastic cup and poured a very large whisky.

'Damn! Damn! Damn!' he said, and lit a cigarette.

He'd spent the whole week while he was trapped in hospital thinking of Sally – well, lusting after Sally, to be strictly accurate. His imagination had had to be doing something while he was marooned frustratingly in bed for a week. Having spent so long trying to convince himself that he wasn't interested he'd allowed himself to go hopelessly the other way and become a touch besotted. He'd convinced himself that they were going to have an affair. He'd even made his preliminary plans and booked a table for Saturday night. And why not? What could be more natural than that they should end up in each other's arms after what they had endured together? It was a relief, he supposed, that he had crashed in on her and Robert before making a fool of himself, but nonetheless he felt cheated. It would have been such fantastic publicity to have had an affair with Sally Blair.

'Oh well,' he sighed to himself in the mirror. 'Win some, lose the bloody rest.'

There was a knock on his door. He didn't answer, he didn't want to speak to anyone. Dawn came in anyway.

'I wondered if you fancied a drink,' she said.

'No thanks. Close the door a sec, will you. Take a seat if you like. How long have Sally and Robert been carrying on?'

'Since last Wednesday. It didn't take her long. Natural enough, I suppose. Robert's got a good hunky shoulder for leaning on.'

'She thinks no one knows about them.'

'Everyone knows, darling. Aren't you going to offer me one of those?'

Philip washed out another cup and poured her a Scotch. He carried it over to the couch, where she had kicked off her shoes and stretched herself out languidly. She was wearing a low-cut silky top and a short skirt which she had made no attempt to prevent from riding up her thighs. Philip paused to admire her legs.

'You're looking rather decadent tonight.'

'You mind?'

Philip thought about it for a moment.

'No.'

He returned to his seat and pretended to be searching on the table for his lighter while actually looking at her legs in the mirror. He'd known her, for what, twenty-five years? Twenty-five years and he'd never made a pass. Quite extraordinary, and most unlike him. He wondered if she had ever been interested.

'You're not jealous of Robert, are you, Philip?'

'Oh of course not. Not remotely. Just wanted to know what was going on, that's all.'

'Good. She's much too young for you, you know.'

'Who is?'

'Sally. You're going to be fifty in a few years, Philip. What are you going to do with a girl of Sally's age? Take her down the disco?'

'I think you're jumping to conclusions, Dawn. Who said I was interested in Sally?'

'The moment you thought she was having an affair with Dick Jones I think you became highly interested.'

'You think I'm that small-minded?'

'I know it for a fact.'

'Well I've a bone to pick with you, Dawn, now you mention it. It's quite possible I made a bit of a fool of myself when I thought Dick had pre-empted me, but why? Why was I so convinced that he and Sally were an item? You know perfectly well why, don't go all wide-eyed on me now, dear. It was because you damned well told me. You told me, for a gospel fact, that Sally had confided in you that she was sleeping with Dick. This was a complete and utter blatant lie. How do you explain yourself?'

'Easily. I didn't want you seducing Sally Blair.'

'Why ever not?'

'Because I wanted you for myself.'

It was an unexpected reply and Philip had no answer to it. He sat inertly, his weight well forward in his chair, gaping at her. She made sure she was quite comfortable before continuing.

'I've fancied you for years, Philip. On and off, it's true; you haven't been my abiding secret passion, nothing silly like that, but I've always carried a bit of a flame for you. And now, to be perfectly frank, I think I've waited long enough, don't you? When we were working down here last time I wondered if anything might happen then, I certainly hoped it would, but you were already having an affair with that slip of a thing who worked in the office. Most aggravating. It's a terrible male weakness, you know, this need as you get older to be seen consorting with girls half your age. It's really time, I think, that I helped save you from yourself.'

'What about Malcolm?'

'Who's Malcolm?'

'Your husband.'

'No, he's called Martin. I've never been married to any-one called Malcolm, at least I don't think so. Martin and I are perfectly happy together, since you mention it. I don't want to divorce him and move in with you, Philip. I just want to go to bed with you.'

'I see.'

'Is that all you're going to say?'

'Oh . . . no.'

'There isn't anyone else, is there?'

'Oh, no, no, no. Unless you count Olive.'

'And do you?'

'Er, no.'

'Then why are you hesitating?'

'I wasn't aware that I was.'

'Oh Philip, this is hopeless. After twenty-five years your bovine obtuseness has finally forced me to forgo any attempt at subtlety and offer myself to you on a plate. I'm not used to this, you know, not at all. Would you please cease being so dim-witted and make an appropriate response?'

'All right. How about – your place or mine?'

'Yes, you're right not to waste any time trying to be original; the corny lines are best. Yours, I think. I hear you've got an incredibly comfortable bed.'

'Who told you that?'

'Sally. You offered it to her, after the first night, remember? Without you in it, but I expect that was only a ploy. Sally tells me everything.'

'And you misrepresent her.'

'But of course. My motives are entirely guided by self-interest. I don't mind being candid about it, because I've always recognized in you a kindred spirit. I'm right, aren't I?'

He acknowledged her perspicacity with a little bow. She took his proffered hand.

'Shall we go?'

They left the theatre together arm in arm, stiff-backed, like a grand old-time performing partnership who've seen and done it all, and know how to take an exit with style and panache. Dawn drove Philip to his flat and he took her immediately to see his incredibly comfortable bed. She liked it so much that she spent practically the rest of the summer in it.